Dragonflies Within

By

Sherie L. Howard

To my daughter
Amanda,
whose first step inspired me
to never stop dancing,
Gvgeyui Forever.

Chapter One

A bright yellow CSX train wiggled its way from Chicago to Detroit,

like a devil's darning needle. The April wind was unforgivingly

cold, birthed by Lake Erie, but not enough to deter Asad Harb from

meeting his only brother. A week earlier, Vermilion, Ohio had been

his meeting spot, the pinpoint location where 930 pounds of

explosives would disappear, right under the nose of the CSX

engineer, an easy assignment for Asad and a few of his comrades,

who swore allegiance to ISIS, like his father in Syria had, until a gunmetal U.S. Army Apache helicopter blew Asad's father to pieces.

Now, Asad would take up where his father left off. The reason for

his continued allegiance to the Islamic State of Iraq and Syria was

simple – revenge against the United States.

He pulled up, lights off, and waited at the corner of South

and State Street until he saw his younger brother Bobby park,

Michigan plates, a small brown 2014 Chevy Silverado. He hated the

fact that his flesh and blood, with the last name of Harb, *war* in

Arabic, a name to be proud of, would own and drive a truck that was

built and put together in the USA, much less one that was already

two years old. Asad got out of his 2016, night-blue Samand Soren,

and walked slowly toward his younger brother, a Detroit

construction worker, weak in his brother's opinion, and *too*

American. Bobby was simple – married, but not happily, no kids,

and saw the last box of available explosives as a chance to make

something of himself. Commercial grade. Enough to get the job

done, with the right planning and organization. Bobby's take was

only twenty-pounds, a small cut of the 930 taken from the Chessie

Seaboard Railroad (CSX), a figure that was twice the amount

reported by the liaison to the media, as instructed by The Federal

Bureau of Alcohol, Tobacco, and Firearms (ATF), a piece of

information the Detroit office would keep under wraps, a decision

made by Associate Deputy Director Aaron Bosman, and something

that would seal the fate of innocent victims across America.

#

Enola May Starks knew the feeling caused by a devil's darning

needle, could detect its long needle-shaped body numbing her fear,

hesitation, and anxiety that had been a part of her since childhood,

multiplied by two failed marriages and the challenges of being a

single mother. It didn't help that she still carried her dead mother's

M, from her first name – Melantha, in her middle name – May.

POKE. She placed her hand on her chest, trying to calm the

endless stir inside of her. FLUTTER. She pictured Allie and Mitch.

Both had grown up without her knowledge, a signal that it was time

to let go of a role she had played too long, that of being a single

mother. Now, it was time for open-highway. She pictured Allie,

living in Quartzsite, Arizona with her fiancé, followed by another

snapshot – this one of Mitch, off the coast of Louisiana, operating a

crane on a lift-boat, somewhere in the Gulf of Mexico. Her grown

children were proof that life was moving faster. She knew time wasn't promised. Her biological father, Grover Starks, was her reminder of that fact, his life taken from him at the bottom of a snowy ravine, courtesy of her mother and a sabotaged brake-line, the same mother that had committed suicide, courtesy of a broken saucer and a severed radial artery in her wrist.

Enola May went to bed that night thinking about the deed her biological father had left her, his only heir, a piece of his past, an abandoned segment of desert, somewhere in Roswell, New Mexico. She smiled at the flutter inside her lower stomach, before nodding off to sleep, before dreaming about Roswell. Pools of blue-green surrounded her. Dust and tan-colored clay made its way into her open car windows, marking her ordinary white shirt and light blue jeans with the soil of western freedom. Imaginary cactus dotted the highway, resting spots for birds that flirted in the desert stillness. A mass of orange, red, and yellow lit the way to Roswell. Then she woke up, as the sound of Florida rain hit the window pane. She felt she was still surrounded by dragonflies of various colors, some fluttering about, their bodies summonsing her. That's when she decided it was time to retire from teaching, time to revisit places from her past, time to explore new places, time to see her adult children, time to see Dixie, time to see Roswell, and time to choose a new life.

May, the last month of teaching tenth graders went by fast. *Liberated* and *accomplished* were two words that had described her every move over the last month. She had sold all her furniture on Craigslist, given Goodwill bits and pieces of her past, and had been living with her dear friend, René, over the last few weeks, since her apartment lease expired, working jigsaw puzzles in the evening, the two of them, fitting oddly shaped pieces together, forming mountains surrounded by wildlife and flowers. It had been a chance for Enola to recharge, spending time with René, smiling, laughing, and sharing thoughts about the future. A chance to do nothing. Until, last weekend, when Enola spent four hours traveling north, to the top of the state, to stash carefully packed Rubbermaid containers of personal items into her rented five-by-five storage unit. The dark blue one, she knew held her most prized possession – a 1967 Dr. Do-Little two-headed stuffed llama that Allie had worked for over a year to find her on eBay – a replacement for the one that had been forcefully pulled away from her, when a U-Haul took her six-year-old life away from Detroit, the city she had known as a young child, and a city she would stand in again on Thursday, the first one in June, and the first planned stop of her travels. She had always been systematic and a planner. *First, I should go back to where things started for me.* She thought. *JAX to Detroit Metropolitan.* But from there, she would play it by heart, for the first time in her life.

Chapter Two

The vacant lot on Lorman Street was now a mixture of dirt,

overgrown grass, broken beer bottles, and large shards from a purple

Crown Royal bottle that glistened in the sunlight, which made the

dandelions that tried to hide behind it appear purple. *Purple*

dandelions. I smiled as I studied them, something beautiful

surrounded by such emptiness. I reached down to pick a dandelion

from the mangled assortment of leaves and broken glass. As I

brought it closer to my face, I remembered my mother. *Suicide at thirty-eight.* I glanced back down, smiling at the leaves from where I had plucked the dandelion. They looked like angry teeth, jaggedly shaped. My mom would be proud that leaves shaped like lions' teeth made me think of her.

I stood there for a moment, taking in the damp Detroit air, before waving to the Uber driver that had been waiting on me, my transportation to the corner of Livernois and Michigan Avenue. Upon arrival, I could see my past had been erased. This time, the hospital where I was born, had been replaced with LA Insurance Company, again I thought of Melantha, imagined that somehow, she had erased my very existence, masterminded from whatever spiritual world she resided in.

I decided to make my way on foot for a while. *I can send for another Uber later.* I thought, then started my long walk down Michigan Avenue. Hungry, I took notice of Mike's Famous Ham Place, where I opened the thick door covered in metal bars and walked in. I sat at the counter, studying the friendly face that waited on me. Weathered. Hardened. But, somewhere in there I saw a glimmer of hope. I wondered if he was the owner, a man who had struggled to keep his business open, despite the graffitied walls just outside his door, despite the drug houses that I had walked by for the last couple of miles, surrounding his business-like enemy soldiers, despite the prostitutes that solicited every full belly that left his restaurant, and despite the lost and broken souls that dotted Michigan Avenue. I could see that his wise eyes still saw the good in people on the other side of his counter. He looked at me like I was a purple dandelion. *Did strangers see good in me?* I questioned.

I was hungry for the plate of fresh-baked ham and over-easy eggs he placed before me, and hungry for whatever knowledge he had of Detroit. I'm sure his customers came from all walks of life. But at the time, they were mostly black or Middle Eastern, and they all looked like they had two things in common – they knew about hard times, and they knew about survival. I didn't feel out of place at that counter; I belonged there.

"Uber won't come here," the woman, who I quickly figured out was his wife, said matter-of-factly. "They never do." She smiled at me. "They don't like coming down here."

"Thanks. I'll figure out something," I answered even though I had no idea where I was headed or how I would get there. Since flying into Detroit, Uber had been my only source of transportation.

"I can give you a ride," said the man, two seats over from me, leather work boots, light amber-colored eyes that almost matched them, and a muscular build.

"No thanks," I answered, and then "but I appreciate the offer."

"Where are you headed?" asked the amber-colored eyes.

"I want to find a place to stay near Baltimore Street, near the Amtrak Station." He looked like a lightning bolt had just hit him between the eyes. I wondered why but didn't ask, allowing him to stare through me. "I'm planning my trip as I go."

"I'm Bobby," and then "I don't mind." I looked at his eyes, considered my options, and imagined purple dandelions pooling in each of his eyes.

"I would appreciate that Bobby." I noticed the wedding ring. *Serial killers are married too.* I reminded myself. And then, "I'm Enola."

"Hey Enola, nice to meet you." He shuffled a napkin in his hand, wiped his mouth, and placed a ten on the counter before waving to the owner and his wife. Bobby and I talked about Detroit, as he drove through sections, that I was happy I wasn't walking in.

We talked about how my childhood hospital and first home were gone.

"Detroit fights every day to hold on," he said. I knew what he meant. It's about the goodness still left in the world – *the purple dandelions* – I thought, as he pulled up to The Viking Motel, someplace that, in my opinion, looked like it rented by the hour, but someplace close to a subway, a casino, city bus stops, and a short distance from Amtrak. I slipped him a ten for his trouble, to replace the one I had seen him leave at Mike's Famous Ham Place. He didn't want to take it, but I insisted.

"The least I can do is pay for your lunch." He smiled at me, as he wrote down his cell number on a piece of scratch paper and handed it to me, my other hand reaching for the door.

"Thanks for saving my life." He said. I just looked back at him, wondering what he meant, but again, I didn't ask.

"You're welcome," I said back before exiting his vehicle. I didn't know what I meant either, but there was a small part of me, that felt he had saved me too.

I spent a couple of days exploring Detroit. I went places I was told not to go. The first, a small restaurant off Seven Mile, had the best fried chicken, black-eyed peas, and macaroni and cheese I'd ever eaten. Standing in line, I was the only Caucasian at the take-out counter, but no one looked at me like I didn't belong there. I studied the people around me – a black man in his sixties with a yellow dress shirt, yellow silk dress pants, and shiny shoes – also yellow – had been watching me.

"Hello." He spoke directly to me.

"Hi. You look very nice today." I tried not to sound too corny, but every inch of him matched perfectly. I could feel his strength, the strength of the people in that room, and the strength of the restaurant itself. Motor City Soul Food wasn't shy about the fact that it served up some of the best soul food cooking in America. The line, take-out only, proved it.

"Thanks, young lady." The yellow man smiled. And then with a curious tone, "Have you been here before?"

"No, I haven't." I knew he wondered how I had discovered a locals-only establishment. "I saw this restaurant on *Diners, Drive-Ins and Dives* with Guy Fieri on television." I thought about Fieri's review. *Best soul food ever.*

"Ain't that something." It was more a statement of fact, than a question. "It is, young lady, it is."

I smiled, happy that he didn't see a dividing line. We continued to small talk, made our way down the counter, and exited the building around the same time, each with a homecooked meal. I carefully balanced the to-go container, in one hand, and reached for my camera phone with the other.

"Don't take photos out here – not on the street," he paused looking at me honestly. "Too many gangbangers out here that will shoot you for that." *Dividing lines.* I thought.

"Thanks," I replied. I could feel the nerves in my face tighten. They stayed tight until my driver appeared, another Uber, not Bobby, even though he had crossed my mind, but then I remembered the wedding ring. Still I imagined him coming to my rescue again, a thought I played over and over in my mind, until I locked the deadbolt at The Viking Motel, and took my first bite of Motor City Soul Food.

The next day I caught a subway to Greek town, walked and explored the main streets there, before sauntering back to The Viking Motel, and before heading across the street to the Motor City

Casino. I had felt the racial tension on the subway and several streets, and wasn't able to relax, until I carried on a thirty-minute conversation with one of the security guards at the casino. He told me that I shouldn't have went to Seven Mile, and he laughed and shook his head when I mentioned I wanted to see Eight Mile – a famous stretch of road, probably because of the movie starring Eminem. I thought about the *Eight Mile* movie, what it represented to me – a dividing line, between races of people. I hated the feeling, so the next morning I called Bobby.

"Hey Bobby, it's Enola." I imagined his wife listening from their living room sofa. "I can't find an Uber driver that is willing to take me down Eight Mile." I paused. "Do you have any free time today?" And then, "I'll cover your gasoline and time." *Business.* I convinced myself.

"I can pick you up at The Viking." He sounded happy I called. Too happy. "In an hour?"

"Thanks Bobby." I tried not to think of his muscular build or amber-colored eyes that danced in my thoughts. "I'll be outside."

I was a passenger in a man's pickup truck that I didn't know. The sunlight followed us, as his right leather work boot operated the gas, occasionally the brake, and seemed to move slowly and deliberately like my thoughts. Eight Mile was a long street of drug houses. Bobby warned me not to take photos, just like the yellow man from Motor City Soul Food, so I didn't. I just stared at the endless string of lost lives and lives in turmoil. Endless.

"Thanks for taking me down here Bobby." I tried not to show how much I desired him as I spoke.

"Why did you want to come?" He slowed the vehicle and glanced in my direction. "Curiosity?" He smiled. "Trying to figure out why some people make certain choices?" He asked. I knew what he meant, although it seemed like a peculiar question.

"I guess I do try to analyze people…and places." I answered, catching his light golden eyes, that seemed to sparkle in the late Detroit sun.

"How would you analyze me?" He asked. I took in the question before wording my answer. Carefully.

"You analyze people too," I answered without answering him. Then, I decided to be more direct. "You're married, lonely, respect human life, mysterious, and yearn for more." I stared out the window, realizing he was already taking me back to The Viking Motel.

"Guilty as charged." He added, as he pulled up to the motel. "I see things in you too." He wanted to tell me. "I see a woman who wants a best friend, someone she can count on, someone that won't lie to her, someone that feels like home." He turned off the engine, waiting for a response, waiting for an invite. I looked at his left hand, eager to ask him to come in, and eager to do many things, but the wedding ring stopped me.

"I'm glad I met you Bobby." Then, with regret, "I hope we meet again…maybe another life." I could tell he did too. I opened the passenger door, exited, and turned back for one last look. I could see the dandelions in his eyes. The purple had darkened.

"You saved my life." He said a second time since we had met, before backing up, before watching me walk into my motel room in his rearview mirror, and before pulling over at the first side street, his crème-colored fingers carefully disconnecting the vest under his shirt, connected to twenty pounds of explosives.

Chapter Three

Enola May Starks didn't know that the bulk of Bobby Harb's muscular build was a vest strapped with explosives, didn't know he had worn it four times since the end of April, didn't know the last two times it had been within inches of her, and didn't know he had slowly taken it off each time, after changing his mind, without detonation, sparing his own life and the others around him. Unknowingly, she boarded an Amtrak train to Buffalo, New York on a Tuesday morning, after taking a ninety-minute bus ride from the

Detroit Amtrak station to Toledo, where she boarded the Buffalo bound train. She didn't know the Amtrak building in Detroit had been one of Bobby's most recent targets, until he met her, and once again realized he would not only be killing himself, but people like her, for a cause he didn't even believe in.

Mesmerized by up-state New York, Enola stared out the large side window of the Amtrak train. Full-bodied trees lined the metal track most of the way to Buffalo, where she was in competition with Justin Bieber fans for a place to stay. It was almost eight p.m. before Enola secured a spot at the Lenox Hotel. Hot, tired, and desperately seeking a room, which the hotel desk obliged.

"Welcome Enola." The desk clerk read the name off her Florida license, treating her like someone she had known for some time.

"Hi, how are you?" Enola questioned the hotel clerk, an attractive figure with a face that had seen hard times, probably in her late twenties. Friendly. Outgoing. Down-to-earth. You could tell.

"I'm great." The name tag reading Leigh answered. "I hope you enjoy Buffalo while you're here. Lots of shops, antique stores, and restaurants one street over on Allen."

"Great. Sound like a nice way to spend tomorrow." Enola smiled as she answered, wishing she knew someone in Buffalo. Anyone.

The next morning, Enola let her soul soak in buildings rich in architectural design, gold-trimmed roofs, triangular-shaped windows, shades of blue, yellow, green and bright candy red. She snapped a photo of a t-shirt in a boutique's window. It simply read: *I miss you. XO.* She sent it to Allie using Facebook Messenger, while thinking about Allie's last text from Arizona. *We went swimming in the river today.* It was a thought that replayed, twenty minutes later, as Enola found herself staring at the Erie Canal, wishing she could go swimming too, to counteract the sun that beat down on her shoulders and the sweat that beaded on her cheeks. The June heat in Buffalo, New York, was more intense than she expected, almost as bad as the heat she imagined beating down on her car that waited in the economy parking lot at the JAX airport in Florida. The heat made her picture Bobby's face, and for a moment she imagined him touching her, anything to soothe the loneliness she was feeling. Her thoughts changed when she took notice of the fighter-ship parked along the canal. Its cold metal swayed in the water, rocking the loneliness inside her gut into a peaceful heartbeat. TICK-TICK. She felt the tip of an unknown wing calm her, as she spied the lighthouse across the canal, a symbol of strength since 1833. *I can do this,* she thought. It was a statement that countered the uneasiness that came with not knowing where she would be a week from now. *Twenty-four hours at a time.* She rationalized.

Tomorrow she would board another Amtrak train to Niagara Falls; it was decided that seeing Niagara Falls and popping over the border into Canada with her new passport was something she could muster. *Might as well.* She smiled at her freedom and the uncertainty of her future, absorbing the nervous flutter breathing inside her gut. Enola imagined herself without a life jacket, bobbing up and down in the cold Erie Canal. She smiled at the visual in her head – her body relaxed, tipping and moving into each gentle wave. She could see the look on her face. It wasn't fear. She smiled at the cold water holding her afloat. It smiled back at her.

The first morning in Niagara Falls, New York, she was up early at Shiva's Traveler's Lodge, dressed comfortably, ankle socks with dark navy sneakers, the outer toed-area a calming green mesh overlay, lightweight and ready to walk. Her five-four frame was dressed in an earthy silk sleeveless shirt and Levi jeans.

The deafening sound of Niagara Falls pulled her thoughts back to the here and now, releasing water that refused to be held hostage, as it poured over the top of the American Falls into the gorge below. It raced 180 feet to its birth in a new body that would set it free in the Atlantic Ocean. Mist and cold water beat lightly on Enola's face. She felt alive, transfixed on watching the American Falls race to the bottom of the gorge, where the Maid of the Mist rocked from its power. Drawn to the boat ride, she welcomed the sting of pounding water on her face and let the roar from the water's belly fill the empty spots in her soul, before deciding to explore the slippery slopes that surrounded the Cave of the Winds. Drenched and exhausted, she made her way by trolley to the Aquarium of Niagara where she stood and watched the harbor seal play for almost an hour. As evening approached, Enola walked to St. Peter's Episcopalian Church, where she studied the doily shaped pattern, the shape of the church's largest window – twelve points. Delicate. Inviting, but a place she preferred not to go. Attending church was by necessity only – a funeral, a wedding, and of course her own children's christenings, when they were babies, just in case there was

a God, although Enola doubted his existence.

Enola turned her attention away from St. Peters and back to

the falls as night approached, deciding to secure a spot to watch the

ten p.m. fireworks, held nightly over the illuminated water. Soon,

she watched the June sky fill with different colors, a distraction to

soothe the endless flutter inside her.

#

The Amtrak train pulled out of Niagara Falls early the next morning.

I was the only one who boarded from that location. It didn't take

long before the train entered Canada, where all passengers were

instructed to get off and go through customs before re-boarding.

Passport. Questions. Re-board.

I watched out the window as I rode on Canada's version of

Amtrak – VIA Rail. The train seemed to move quicker than Amtrak,

but it passed lives that were the same as those in the United States.

Boys playing basketball, men swinging golf clubs, women pushing

shopping carts, and young girls running on a soccer field, all played

like a movie, as I stared out the side window of the train. The VIA

Rail passed a Target, a Red Lobster, a Ford dealership, a Sears, and a hospital. I could see how human we all were, just by watching out the pane of glass that separated me from the world. I thought about how I always tried to appreciate the differences among cultures and people, unlike the hands that had raised me – Dacey and Melantha Fears. I also thought about what I had failed to do – appreciate how we were all the same. We all wanted happiness, peace, families, good health, and laughter. I took a deep breath thinking about happiness, until I could no longer block-out the conversation around me, about Sunday night, last night, about senseless death. The men, deep in conversation behind me, were angry, disturbed by the fact that someone could be so cruel. I sat frozen. Listening. A nightclub. People shot for no reason. Forty-nine innocent lives taken. Then, I heard them say the name of the state where I had lived for almost forty years. Florida. Tears fought loose from the corners of my eyes. BITE.

#

Umar MaHaz knew the Harb brothers in Detroit. He also knew their differences; which in his opinion were perfect examples of strength and weakness. *Now you, Umar you've got a chance to do what's right. Like Asad.* He played his friend's words over and over in his head, before walking into the nightclub, the tenth of June, in Tampa, carrying an assault rifle, a handgun, and ten pounds of explosives, the latter, part of a shipment his friend had purchased from Asad Harb in Detroit. He knew he wouldn't be coming out alive. *Strength.* Looking death in the face, he sprayed bullets into the souls of over a hundred people, innocent victims, taking half of them to their graves. His actions trickled down family-trees, altering the lives of thousands; he snuffed out living, breathing, human beings, in a place where music healed and acceptance replaced oxygen. Bobby Harb felt ashamed. He knew ISIS was responsible. He didn't want to be like Umar, an instrument in destruction, the cause of blood splatter, and the deliverer of evil. In fact, it was Bobby who was comforted, after reading how officers ended the attack, taking Umar's final breath with a bullet.

#

I was still thinking about the innocent lives lost, as the train came to a stop in downtown Toronto. The city was made of glass. Windows sparkled, and floor after floor towered above the city, making me anxious to explore its every curve and corner, but it would have to wait until morning. Tonight, I would make it to a hotel, where I would instant message Allie on Facebook and chat with Mitch on WhatsApp. They were all I had, a fact that weighed heavily, after listening to the story about the nightclub shooting. I wanted to make sure they knew, what I was sure they already knew. *I love you.* I thought about those three little words, thought about what they meant to me, and thought about how I had spent my childhood hoping for those words from the people I had for parents. *Gvgeyui.* I remembered how Dacey Fears' mother would say her Cherokee Indian version of *I love you* to my half-sister, and how she was careful to never say it to me, the unwanted child, so I made sure my children knew before letting my head hit the pillow at the Toronto Airport West Hotel, where darkness surrounded me.

The following morning came earlier than I expected. Sunlight shined through the fourth story window into my hotel room in Mississauga, Ontario, close to where I boarded the Union Pearson Express. The U.P. took me to the city of glass, the beautiful city of Toronto. I spent most of the day walking city blocks, exploring shops, and being frugal. My recent retirement made me take extra notice of my expenses – but not tonight. I took the elevator up to the one-hundred and sixteenth floor of the CN Tower, where I ate salmon and chocolate lava cake. Afterward, I went one more floor

up, to the observation deck, where the darkened sky blew wind in

my hair. The lights below twinkled. Appearing far-off, unreachable,

like so many things in life. The comparison seemed to mock tragedy,

the illusion that it was kept at a distance. *It's not.* I assured my

thoughts. *Devastation has a far reach.* The thought seemed to stay

with me throughout the night, and followed me to the airport the

next morning, before landing with me on the tarmac, at LaGuardia

Airport in New York.

Chapter Four

Enola had a ten-hour layover at the LaGuardia Airport, time enough,

even with the heaviest traffic she'd ever seen to make it by shuttle to

Tower One in Manhattan. Ground Zero. Enola thought about the day

the world fell apart in New York. *September 11, 2001.* Both towers

hit. *What type of human being would fly a commercial airplane into*

a building intentionally? She felt tears making their way down her

face as she ran her hand over the names carved into bronze, a sign of

permanence in a world where nothing is permanent. *Why?* Then she questioned her own country, as she thought about the Enola Gay, her namesake, its belly opening to drop the atomic bomb on Hiroshima. *What gave us the right to kill innocent people in Hiroshima?* She studied the massive reflecting pools outside Tower One with tears in her eyes. *Men play God every day, deciding who lives and who dies.* She felt sick as she summarized her feelings.

Walking the High Line seemed like the only way to find some peace again. Mitch had mentioned it on the app they were using to keep in touch, his cell phone no longer activated, an attempt to be less available in Enola's opinion. Mitch had changed. The crooked smile he would model as a young boy and early teen had diminished, an observation that radiated through her, as she walked slowly on the High Line, soaking in the sunshine, and playing out the next portion of her trip in her head. *Dixie.* The thought made her anxious to get back to the JAX Airport, find her car in economy parking, and drive. *I'll plan a few days at a time.* It seemed like a reasonable compromise, a striking difference in comparison to the orderly life she had lived for so long.

Enola picked up pace, as she walked the almost two-mile-long route, elevated over Manhattan. It was lined with flowers of every color, well-manicured shrubbery, and offered a beautiful view of where the NYC Central Railroad once roared down metal tracks that still peeked up from the asphalt path. She inhaled a deep breath of flowers and sunshine, after reading a freshly painted billboard with a catchy slogan: *Peace starts in your heart.* She wondered if the world would ever find peace.

#

It seemed that crime followed me, a feeling I couldn't shake as I scrambled over the mountains into Asheville. I was happy it was the middle of the summer – June – no snow. I didn't want to travel the same snowy highway that saw my father's last day of life. Today it was a sweltering eighty-five, although less humidity than Florida, with clear roads.

Dixie looked great for fifty-five years old. Her husband Ryan was at work, still running the same company, his father once ran – Asheville Gas, and still being a committed husband in their almost thirty-five-year marriage. *Wow, has it been that long?* I calculated the lifetimes that had come and gone. *Childhood, plus marriage one, plus marriage two, plus raising Mitch and Allie, plus retiring.* I smiled a tired grin, my lips slightly parting, as I carefully maneuvered around her two lab puppies, then after reevaluating their size – *dogs*.

"I've missed you sister." Dixie greeted me in her southern accent, something I was capable of imitating in Asheville, North Carolina when I was a kid, and something I had lost when I moved away at fifteen.

"Dixie, I've missed you so much." I smiled as I hugged her. "Sisters forever girl."
My comment made me think of April Lynn, my half-sister that I hadn't seen in almost forty years. Several lifetimes.

"You look great." Dixie pulled away from me to give me the once over.

"You do too." Her life looked great: a beautiful house on a piece of property, a wonderful husband, and two big dogs that adored her.

"I'm so glad you're here." She said. "I was hoping you would spend some time with me before heading to Arkansas to see our boy." I remembered I had told her five or six hours back, on the phone, that I would probably head to Mitch next, that I had never been to Arkansas, where he was now living, and that I welcomed spending even one day with him. Then I thought about how I had

made Dixie and Ryan Durrant the Godparents to Mitch and Allie,

something their dad didn't particularly like, something that reminded

him that his Italian heritage had failed him, leaving him without

choices, without cousins to leave his children to in the event of an

emergency. Dixie and Ryan were my idea.

"I'm glad I'm here too." I didn't tell her that I hated the

Asheville mountains, the ones that had killed my grandmother, had

robbed me of my existence in Motor City, had hidden the man that

beat me as a child, had magnified my mother's delusions and

assisted in her suicide, and had painted a snowy path to my

biological father's death. I could feel them towering around me,

trying to hold me prisoner in a place that never felt like home.

By the middle of the week, and the last Wednesday in June,

we had driven down familiar streets and past my childhood home

several times, no longer a threat, the front yard filled with the

laughter of two small boys running through a carefully placed

sprinkler, the father twirling the youngest around, and the mother

bringing out a picture of Kool-Aid to the nearby picnic table. *It's not

the place. It's the people.* I corrected my thoughts. And by week's end, the feeling of being smothered disappeared. The mountains seemed smaller, less threatening.

"Drive carefully." She said the words as a friend, and as a sister. "Thanks for hanging with me Nola." I thought about how long it had been since anyone had called me Nola. I couldn't remember.

"I will Dix." I gave her a long hug, before I got in my car, and backed away from memories that had seemed so dark over the last forty years. Slowly, I left what had always felt like the scene of a crime, working my way along Old Leicester Road, and finally in the direction of I-40 West, to a future I couldn't see, but I didn't let the rearview mirror haunt me anymore.

The North Carolina mountains quickly became Tennessee mountains. Stopping in Harrison, just before Knoxville, at a small park, I got out, camera in hand, snapping photos of butterflies, vines that trailed up large oaks, and wildflowers. A young woman, in her mid-twenties, handed money to the passenger of a car parked near mine, my attention fixed on the scene, as I made my way back to my car. As I got closer, I could see desperation covered her face, as the driver of the car she had been standing by backed away. Quickly. Her attempt to hold onto the passenger's car-door failed, sending her to the ground. For a moment, I considered running toward her, assisting her, and making sure she was okay, but my reactions changed when, like a bad movie, a man standing ten feet behind her, assumed a shooting stance and began firing at the car as it sped away. Pow. Pow. Pow. Pow. Too close for comfort, and nervous about stray bullets, I hid behind the largest oak I could find. *Drug deal gone bad.* I assumed. I stayed hidden until the ripped-off couple exited, leaving in their car, in quick pursuit of the other car, which appeared long gone. I made it to my car after the coast was clear, passing a jogger who was already on his phone to the police. *Just drive*, I thought to myself. Still rattled by the sound of gunfire, I made my way to I-40 West.

#

Daronté Smith fit the build of the young man with the gun in Harrison Park, but not the race, still, police were certain his car matched the description. A rusty sedan. That's when two police cars whipped on their lights, pulling the nervous black male to the side of the highway, and ordered him from his car, with their guns drawn. Sweat beaded on the young man's dark skin, and in the pit of his stomach, as life stood still. Daronté did as instructed, his hands extended above his head, turning his back to the officers, and slowly walking backward. The vibration closest to his heart was his cell phone he imagined, and without thinking he brought his right hand down from the hot air. Bullets knocked his phone to the pavement, his mother pleading for her son to answer, but the next voice she heard belonged to Officer Davison. Her son, a twenty-four-year-old college student, lay lifeless on the side of I-40, in a pool of bright red asphalt.

Chapter Five

Enola had seen the sirens as she sat in traffic. She imagined it was an accident that had backed up I-40 for hours, delaying her goal of making Memphis, but determined she continued driving, after traffic cleared, eerily slow.

The first of July sky was a dark shade of night by the time she parked her car at the Bass Pro Shop below the bridge, hiding everything except what appeared to be the outline of an Egyptian pyramid. Sleep came easy in the parking lot full of campers, and morning seemed to wake her with a gentle shake, the light rainstorm leaving a trail of red, blue, green, and yellow in the sky – nature's arch. Enola found herself happy, waking to a rainbow, a sign she was headed in the right direction. She knew she would make Little Rock by late afternoon, in time to get an overdue pedicure and manicure. She wanted to look nice when she saw Mitch on the third day of July. *One more day*, she reminded herself.

#

I pulled up to the address where Mitch was staying, his father's residence, and the address he had given me on WhatsApp, ten minutes earlier. The tears started to flow the moment I saw him, his five-foot-eight frame making his way to my car, determined to hug me as he approached my driver's door.

"You look great Ma. I've missed you." He pulled away and directed the words into my blue eyes, the ones that matched his, and the same ones that matched my dead mother.

"I've missed seeing you Mitch." I realized my face was wet. Tears unable to be held, I continued. "I love you so much."

"I love you too Ma." I loved the way he always called me Ma. Over the last couple of years, even following months of lost communication, whenever he texted he used the word Ma in his texts. I would always smile knowing that was him.

The day went way too fast. We stopped for lunch, the time lost between us narrowed, the result of great conversation, cheeseburgers, and large mango smoothies. I missed the days I knew had been easier for him: soccer, football, and his middle school friends. I knew his life had seen its share of ups and downs, relationships lost, job changes, and recently, relocating to another part of the country. It was obvious that he hadn't found his footing as an adult; his normalcy was still being formed. I thought about how everyone's normal is different, but I also knew whatever range of normal he best fit in, was lacking in his life.

We spent the next five hours laughing, talking, and walking side-by-side at the Little Rock Zoo. We stopped at every display, searching for the animal that seemed to enjoy hiding as a challenge, watching its behavior, and laughing at the traits we found similar to our own. July in Little Rock was brutal; heat pounded our faces and necks. One hundred and five degrees registered on my odometer when I cranked the car back on. Hot. We headed to the downtown marketplace for the evening. A mixture of unique shops, out-of-the-ordinary restaurants, and a spectacular view of the Arkansas river entertained us as we continued to catch up on lost time.

"Congratulations on your retirement, Ma." He meant it you could tell. "I hope you end up somewhere that you like."

"Thanks Mitch. I'm glad I did it, but it's nerve-racking not knowing where I'm going to end up, and even scarier not knowing if I'm going to be okay financially." He was twenty-six years old and knew about financial struggles now.

"Do you get the full retirement benefits even though you left before teaching thirty years?" He asked while watching the crowd of people gather near the river walkway.

"Yes, I taught twenty-six years, so the State of Florida pays me that pension, and Pasco county makes up the difference for the other four years. And, I have health insurance." I noticed the crowd was getting larger. "It's just that a pension is about half of what I'm used to living on."

"Oh, wow, that's a big cut." He gently pulled me aside, away from five or six people that were walking, quickly, cell-phones out and in use.

"I know. I've got to get used to it." And then, "I'll get settled somewhere and get a part-time job." I figured out what the crowd was doing, remembering what I had seen my last evening in Niagara Falls. "They're playing that new Pokémon App." I laughed.

"You're kidding?" He smiled. "Remember when I used to collect those cards as a kid?" He questioned with that innocent look I missed so much.

"I'll never forget," I answered wishing the days of innocence lasted longer for all of us. "I miss those days."

"I do too, Ma."

#

Enola pulled into Oklahoma's Boathouse District, around three in the afternoon, the sides of the street already lined with lawn chairs and blankets. She passed food truck after food truck, making the rest of the way on foot, toward the live music, a mixture of country and rock. She stopped to watch a group of teens play cornhole, tossing small bags of corn into a hole at the end of a platform, the lanky blond screaming in excitement at her last toss.

"That's three-points mother fucker." Her voice carried, forgetting there were smaller children around. "That's over twenty-one for me, asshole."

"I'll kick your ass in the next round." The dark-haired boy stammered.

The banter made Enola think of Allie and Mitch, their endless competitions, before Mitch moved out, and before games like cornhole were replaced with dating and working. The reminiscing made her appreciate the darkness that was setting in, serving as a cover-up for her face that couldn't hide missed moments. She braced herself for impact: an hour where silence wasn't an option, an endless multitude of color filled the sky, in uncontrollable spasms that bounced among the stars, like a long overdue orgasm. She could feel herself getting caught up in the moment, as she yearned for a human touch and passion. Her lower abdomen tightened. SHAKE. It wasn't until most of the families around her had left, that she finally stood, and walked back to the parking area, along the street. She tried to convince herself that being alone on the Fourth of July was okay, as she crawled into the back of her vehicle and fought sleep, letting the sound of residential fireworks fill her emptiness.

The next morning, she made her way to Oklahoma's National Memorial & Museum. It seemed surreal when she watched the news about the bombing on television, twenty-one years earlier, when she was pregnant with Allie, watched in horror as the Alfred P. Murrah Federal Building in downtown Oklahoma was surrounded by police and emergency crews trying to pull people from an explosion, a violent blast ignited by a man who was angry with the government. Her immediate reaction was to move her hand down the front of her stomach, touching the outline of her unborn child, as reporters announced that a daycare was in the bottom of the federal building. *How could anyone kill innocent children?* She remembered asking the question. Remembered the facts. *The explosion killed 168 people. Nineteen of them were children.* Enola played the words in her head over and over after walking through the museum and learning the details. *168.* She thought of Allie; she thought of the poor woman who died with her unborn child inside of her. It was considered a domestic terrorist attack by the government; the bomber shared Enola's skin color and citizenship. *A white American.*

Her thoughts swirled, as she listened to a middle-aged father standing near the exhibit, listened to him describe the bomber to his kids, their young impressionable ages soaking in his information.

"He was a terrorist." The young eyes looked up at their father as he spoke.

"Like a Muslim Daddy?" The seven-year-old boy waited for an answer.

"Yes." The father reassured. "Like a Muslim." Enola waited for clarification. Waited for the father to explain how the perpetrator was a white American; instead, he left his children with the visual – a foreign entity – a go-to target group.

"Or, like a black or Mexican person." The daughter, probably ten, whispered to her younger brother, assuring him that white people don't commit horrible crimes.

Enola stood, frozen in time, the air filled with hatred, her mind grasping to understand the racial profiling that is passed down from generation to generation. She thought about Dacey Fears, the man she had known as her father, and how he hated people based on skin color or cultural differences. She wanted to scream. *He was a white American.* But, she didn't. She felt defeated, even though she knew Timothy McVeigh was an ex-United States soldier, a privileged white man, whose heart was hardened by the white supremacist movement. It was those white hands that drove a truck full of explosives to the Oklahoma City Federal Building in April of 1995. White hands. *Evil doesn't know color.* She thought, before exiting the memorial. *Evil isn't a cultural inheritance.*

A few hours later, Enola was eating vermicelli with chicken, beef, shrimp, carrots, and cucumber at Lido's Vietnamese Restaurant in Oklahoma City. She looked around the restaurant, allowing herself to be immersed in culture. *Fuck dividing lines.* She took a deep breath, calming the endless flutter inside, before leaving the solitude she was enjoying, and returning to open road, the only place Enola felt safe.

Chapter Six

The Friday prayer only lasted two cycles. Bowing, kneeling,

prostrating. Bowing, kneeling, prostrating. The holy-day invigorated

his soul and restored his faith in Muslim brotherhood. After

completing the two series of rakats, Bobby Harb stood, reaching

down for the silk, olive-green, prayer rug, called *sajada* in Arabic,

depicting a picture of the Al-Aqsa Mosque in Jerusalem. He rolled it

gently, privately reviewing his promises, first, to be a better husband,

and second, to no longer toy with the idea of ending his own life as a suicide bomber. It was a burden lifted. No longer having to stand in his brother's shadow. He exited the mosque, off Cass Street in Detroit, around one in the afternoon, renewed, no longer having the desire to hurt anyone, not that he ever did, and each step he took down Cass made his heart feel lighter, until a single bullet silenced the merciful heartbeat. The sajada seemed to unroll in mid-air, landing with the top of the rug facing the same direction it had inside the mosque, the direction of Mecca. Bobby's amber-colored eyes stayed closed, his blood-soaked into the olive-green tapestry, as people stopped to stare at his lifeless body, onlookers' faces slowly processing the too-familiar scene, on another Detroit sidewalk. A 2016, night-blue Samand Soren leisurely moved by. Witnesses didn't take notice.

#

It was 105 degrees when she reached Wichita. Determined to find the building of the first Pizza Hut ever opened, Enola put the heat aside, snapping a few pictures and taking a quick walk around the small brick building which no longer operated, before using her GPS, again, this time to locate The Keeper of the Plains, a forty-four-foot statue of an Indian. She sat for about thirty minutes staring at him, a huge metal structure, a representation of protection over things that were important. *We need more like him.* She smiled at the thought, about superheroes and how society could use more real-life heroes to make the world safer.

Hunger and exhaustion sat in as she drove further, stopping in Selina, Kansas for barbecue and making it to Concordia to watch the Kansas sun melt into a field of wildflowers behind a twenty-four-hour Walmart. She would sleep there and figure out tomorrow in the morning. *One moment at a time.* She thought. *I guess that's how I'm living my life until I figure things out.* She replayed her thoughts until sleep took over.

The next day she pulled into the sleepy town of Columbus, Nebraska, where she searched out a reputable full-service auto place – Columbus Tire, and went inside.

"Excuse me sir, do you have a special for an oil, filter, and rotation?" She studied the man on the employee side of the counter. Fifty-six or fifty-seven, hard-worker, looked honest. And then, wedding ring. Dammit. *Why do the good ones always have a wedding ring?* She thought of the gold band on Bobby's finger in Detroit. *Always my luck.*

"Sure. I can get you out the door for thirty-five dollars today." He looked at her. His grin had already evaluated that she was traveling, and had already determined that she wasn't a local. "What's your destination?"

"North, then west." She knew she sounded evasive, but wasn't sure of her next location. She imagined she had that unsettled, displaced look on her face. "Is there anywhere to eat within walking distance while you work on my car?" She guessed it didn't matter now. She might as well let the cat out of the bag. *I'm displaced. I'm hungry. You have a wedding ring.* She hoped he couldn't read all her thoughts.

"Picket Fence Café two blocks down has some mean coconut crème pie." *Maybe he can read my thoughts.*

"Sounds wonderful." Enola smiled.

"Should be ready in about an hour."

"Thanks." She smiled again before walking to the Picket Fence Café. *The coconut crème pie is delicious.* She had the silent conversation with herself, as she devoured each bite. Slowly. Then walked back to Columbus Tire to retrieve her car, before continuing

her journey, and before leaving another married man behind.

She passed Ta-Ha-Zouka Park on 81 North, but quickly u-

turned, her heart desiring the tranquility of the pond, grassy banks,

and shooting waterspout. The silence soothed her and gave her the

burst of energy she needed to keep driving, until the slice of pie wore

off, and hunger sat in. Again. She pulled over at a small wooden

restaurant, a hidden treasure, still off 81 North.

"I'll take the hamburger with macaroni and cheese." She

pointed to the photo in the menu.

"It's really good," said the young waitress, Allie's age.

"Homemade mac-n-cheese with bacon, piled on top of the patty and

covered with a bun."

It sounded like a science experiment, but Enola wanted it.

"I'm brave enough to try it." Enola laughed.

"You won't be sorry." She smiled. And, minutes later, Enola

knew she was right. It was delicious. Enola read through a pamphlet

on the table as she devoured the hamburger with mac and cheese.

Fork required. There was no easy way to pick up a burger loaded with another meal. A piece of bacon crunched inside her mouth before the young waitress returned. "Do you like it?" She asked.

"It's yummy." She smiled hoping her teeth weren't wearing the evidence. "Do you know anything about the prairie arboretum?" Enola asked and pointed to the brochure she had been reading.

"It's about eight miles down the road." She informed Enola. "It's a large park, about forty acres I believe, with all kinds of roses and plants to look at." She picked up Enola's empty plate. "It's relaxing."

"Thanks," Enola replied. "Good food and good advice." Then she smiled as the waitress placed her check in front of her. There was something Enola admired about people who did their jobs and didn't seem to hate them. The waitress was one of those people. Enola tipped her twenty percent and headed down the road.

The prairie arboretum was peaceful. Enola walked the pathway lined with flowers: white, pink, and red roses; Lazy Susans and other types of daisies; and wildflowers in every color. As she walked to her car, she noticed the sun coming down fast in the tall fields to the west. It was time to find a spot to sleep. She wanted to drive her car into the middle of a cornfield and sleep away from the rest of the world, but she knew that wasn't something she could get away with. She noticed three deer run into the endless acres of corn as she passed. The sun folded over them, tucking them in for the night like a mother does to her children. Enola missed hers, missed tucking them in, a vision that stayed with her until she made it to Vivian, South Dakota, where she parked in the corner of a hotel lot, and routinely crawled onto the futon waiting for her.

#

When I got to Oacoma, South Dakota the next morning, I noticed a campground billboard advertising a hot-shower. Five dollars later I felt much better. My hair smelled like coconut milk again, and my breath smelled like mint. Refreshed. I knew I could make it to Badlands National Park in time to enjoy it for the day.

I didn't have to pay the fifteen-dollar admittance fee, as I had ordered and received an *America The Beautiful* ID card before leaving Florida. I smiled at the lady who scanned my card and told me to have a nice time. After driving about a quarter-mile, I noticed three large longhorn sheep grazing on a hill. Too far away for my cheap Android camera to capture them, so I pulled over and simply stared. They looked like skillful leaders – standing strong, sturdy, and purposeful. I followed the winding road, deliberately slow, and took in as much of the landscape as humanly possible. *Breathe.* I had to remind myself. *Relax.* A colorful dragonfly toyed with the outside of my car window, almost keeping pace, diving up and down with the mountainous terrain. I lost sight of him when I stopped the car to take a photo of a deep set of caverns. *Wow.* I thought. *This is beautiful.* I must have gotten out of my car at least a half a dozen times over the next two hours, snapping photos, and standing in awe. I pulled aside to capture a photo of prairie dogs playing with each other, and minutes later, I was lucky enough to see a large pronghorn antelope. He didn't pay attention to me as I snapped several photos. Beautiful. The car wiggled its way up and down ravines and caverns, down dirt roads, and paved ones. By the end of the loop, my red Hyundai was tan-colored, more than red. And as I exited Badlands National Park, I felt grounded – again. No more FLUTTERS.

Chapter Seven

Enola May Starks looked up at the four large faces: Washington, Jefferson, Roosevelt, and Lincoln. It was larger than she expected, noses carved to perfection, and Theodore's glasses were sitting on his face exactly like she had remembered seeing in history books. Mount Rushmore National Memorial was worth the twisting and turning that led from Rapid City to Keystone, not that the scenic drive wasn't worth it on its own merit. After walking the curvy trails at the base of the monument, Enola stopped for an ice-cream – butter pecan. The small shop was on the memorial's property and advertised how their ice cream followed Thomas Jefferson's 1780s recipe for the first ice cream ever made. It was delicious; you could tell by the way she scraped the plastic spoon against the bottom of the container. Five-dollars well spent.

Next stop, was the Crazy Horse Memorial. It was actually going to be larger than Mount Rushmore – someday – that is when it gets finished. Enola stood there looking up at the work that had been done since 1948 and wondered what her own life would be like when she finally completed it. *Will I leave something behind that people will remember?* She wondered. The family that was managing the task of its completion was following the wishes that had been handed down – no government aid. Instead they relied on people like Enola to pay admission, buy lunch, and maybe grab a souvenir on the way out. Enola thought about how some people dedicate their entire lives to a cause. *What cause have I dedicated my life to?* She wondered, but then stopped.

She was too close to Custer State Park, not to check it out. *Maybe I'll see buffalo.* She thought as she drove the eight miles to the park's entrance. It was about fifteen minutes after she entered the park, that she spotted a large buffalo, his feet planted solidly, on the top of a wooded mountainside. Again, a scene that was too far away for a photo, but Enola could clearly see his tail raise in the air, serving as a warning sign that she should stay in her car. The dusty red Hyundai moved slowly by, hoping for a closer view next time one was spotted, but another wasn't spotted, just twisting, turning, steep, windy roads offering a view that would take anyone's breath away. Enola savored every minute, which quickly turned to several hours, before finding her way out of the park and minutes from Pactola Dam and Reservoir. South Dakota definitely showed its beauty around each and every turn.

Enola didn't feel it very often, but she felt it then, as she sat in front of the Pactola Reservoir, she sensed the presence of another source of energy, breathing deep inside of her, its lifeform creating feelings that were too strong to ignore. Secret thoughts stirred, as she analyzed the agitated turmoil, accepting the fact that some people are evil, even unsuspecting faces, and then, she took it one step further, questioning her capabilities. She suspected there was an evil side to everybody, a hidden part, unknown to family and friends. Logic told her that humans were no different than animals. Both kill for survival and both kill for fun. Enola thought about the article she had read a couple years back in a biology magazine, the one about how a scientist proved that the gentleness of a bottlenose dolphin can change in an instant. Out of boredom, a bottlenose dolphin will bite a porpoise, and then head-butt it repeatedly, breaking the porpoise's ribs, watching, waiting for the right time, before making a final blow to the liver. Systematic. Death. A random target.

The image jogged her memory, the hidden visual of a stray cat, one she had seen at a park in Florida, and one that she had witnessed pounce a helpless sparrow. At first, she thought nothing of it, knowing the sparrow would probably get away, then when it became obvious that the sparrow was no longer able to fly, Enola convinced herself the stray cat was probably hungry. She sat at the park bench, unable to take her eyes away, trying to understand, the cat's rapid kicking of its back legs, tossing the small sparrow around like a ragdoll, breaking its neck, and then quickly leaving the scene. The memory haunted her. *Am I capable of violence? Is everybody?*

She wanted to see more buffalo, and after studying a map that she pulled up on her phone, she realized that the Theodore Roosevelt National Park in North Dakota was her best bet. Surely there would be more buffalo there. Maybe if she stared at enough buffalo, she could figure out what keeps those with mass and strength from hurting others. But, tonight, she was too tired for much more driving, not to mention more analyzing. And, there were only two more hours of daylight, just enough time to grab a taco and soda at John's Taco in Deadwood and find a hotel parking lot in Sturgis, where she would dream of animals and people being more alike than most people care to admit.

#

That evening, Asad Harb paced his living room floor. The Nice attack was still all over the news, yet there was very little mention about the explosives found inside the box truck. He brushed it off, knowing that reporters weren't privy to every little detail, especially when it involved an ongoing investigation. He imagined they had seized the thirty-pounds of explosives, investigators working hard to determine where they originated. He smiled. It didn't matter that they didn't reach the center of the Bastille Day celebration. What mattered was the question that was on every official's mind at the local ATF office. *Were the explosives part of the shipment from the CSX train?* Asad knew they were. He knew there were five containers of ammonium nitrate on the cargo ship that left New York only two weeks ago, a much larger amount than Asad could take credit for. Still, he had been notified when his contribution, thirty-pounds of commercial explosives, had been picked up in Le Havre, France. And, he knew it had been his explosives that were inside the truck that claimed eighty-six lives.

#

On top of a mountain in the Theodore Roosevelt National Park in North Dakota, I backed in my car, turned my lights off, and killed the engine, where hidden in the darkness, I stretched out on the futon in the back, with the closest window down about six inches, so I would be able to catch an uninhibited view of the canyons and river that snaked below. A brisk breeze blew over the top of the tall prairie grass that danced to my left. I was in the middle of nowhere, and lucky to have phone reception at all, but I knew I did, as Allie called me in a panic.

"Mom, where are you? North Dakota, right?" She waited for an answer, but I could tell she wanted it immediately.

"Yes, I'm near Watford City. I just parked at the top of Theodore Roosevelt National Park." I paused. "Allie, it's so beautiful."

"You need to keep your doors locked." She knew I always did, but I could tell by the worry in her voice that she had heard something on the news that would mean I should be extra careful.

"What happened?" I wondered who was being targeted now.

"A woman went missing from Fort Totten. I saw her photo on the news. She's so pretty mom." She paused, trying to control her worry. "She reminded me of you."

"Fort Totten is about four hours from me, but I promise I'll be safe Allie." She knew I would, but it didn't stop the worry. We talked about the woman's photo. She was more Allie's age than mine, but she did sound beautiful, her smile, her olive complexion, that I didn't have, but her Indian ancestry that I did. She wasn't part Cherokee like me, she was a Sioux Indian, only twenty-seven years old, her last name was Yellow Bird, bright and happy, like her smile in the photo that Allie described. Disappeared. Gone.

I looked out at the canyon and river after hanging up my cell phone. The land was so beautiful, ravines carved and swayed into each other. That's when I noticed the slow movement of gentle giants. I quickly counted them. Eight. They stood without faltering on the side of a mountain, planted and fearless. *Do they kill for sport also?* I questioned.

Closing my eyes to the world, I listened to the sound of crickets and wind, thinking of the woman's name – Carla Yellow Bird. I prayed to the universe that she would be found safely before falling asleep. It was just after three in the morning, when I woke to a snort just outside my window, its giant mass seemed to stare at me, and then slowly moved away. I watched dark chocolate brown with tufts of unorganized hair fade away from my car, in streaks of the North Dakota moonlight, until the darkness swallowed its outline.

#

Enola May crossed the Montana state line shortly after stopping at The Patriot for a shower, bite to eat, and one load of laundry. She left with coconut-scented hair, a full belly, and clean clothes. A small sign welcomed her into Montana, and an even smaller sign explained the white crosses on the side of the road. It simply read: *The white crosses represent driving fatalities. Drive Carefully.*

Without meaning to, she kept count over the next forty or fifty miles. There was almost one cross for every mile she drove. Forty-six. She wondered how it was possible to have so many fatalities on such an open road. *Had drivers simply fallen asleep?* Then she noticed an Indian reservation to her left. Five miles later, she passed another one. Shortly after, she passed a billboard created by the local Indian council. It read: *We want you to live a long life. If you have a drug or alcohol problem, get help.*

She thought about the different demons inside of people, the **Dragonflies Within**: alcoholism, drug addiction, anxiety, worry, eating disorders, compulsive gambling, racism, sexual addictions, depression, and the hardest to understand, pure evil. It wasn't just some of the Indians near Poplar, Montana that had demons. Demons were everywhere, in every culture, and in every race. She put her hand on her chest, searching for the flutter that was usually there, but she didn't feel it. Not now; but she knew she had her own demons, her own dragonflies – insecurity, fear, anger, loneliness, worry, and never feeling like she was enough. Driving was her therapy. Endless road connecting to endless road. So, she drove for as long as she could on 2 West.

Chapter Eight

A light lit inside Enola May, as she pulled into Shelby, Montana.
Refreshed. She ordered a shredded chicken burrito lunch special
from the waitress at the El Tenampa off Roosevelt Highway, a
chance for small talk.

"Do you like living here?" Enola questioned the friendly
thirty-year-old face that took her order at the El Tenampa
Restaurant.

"Yes. It's nice." She smiled. "No traffic. Friendly." And then, "Where are you from?"

"Florida," Enola answered. "I'm Enola. I retired from teaching, and now I'm looking for a new place to live."

"It's nice here." And then she added, "I'm Magnolia." She looked at Enola trying to size up her age. "Do you have kids?"

"They're grown." And then Enola added, "My son lives in Arkansas, and my daughter is in Arizona with her boyfriend . . . fiancé," she corrected, after remembering.

"You should consider Shelby." She smiled. "It's safe. And, there are some nice single men that come in my other job – The Frontier." She had read Enola's mind. Safe. Check. Available men. Check.

It was just the conversation Enola needed before continuing on her journey. She needed someone to remind her that she wasn't homeless, just displaced, and there were places like Shelby, Montana where she could start a new life, with someone special.

Her mind refreshed, Enola thought about Glacier National Park, thought about the miles ahead of her, and became confident she could make it before dark. She did. She pulled into the Two

Medicine entrance. Finding her way quickly to the lake that faced

the continental divide, Enola parked her car and made her way to a

campground restroom. No showers. Brushing her teeth would have

to do. She made her way back to the car, cracked each window about

an inch, not because she was afraid, but because it was raining hard.

She located her two blankets and searched underneath the futon for a

third. She wasn't used to temperatures dropping into the forties at

night, not near the end of July. She didn't move until daylight. At

seven-a.m. it was only forty-six degrees. She made her way to the

restroom again, pulled out a sweatshirt to slide over her head, and

down over the black cotton tee-shirt she had been wearing. Jeans and

two shirts still weren't enough. She searched the middle of the car,

behind the front console, to find gloves, a knit burgundy cap, and a

black zip-up London Fog jacket, that she had gotten on sale at Ross

several months ago, just in case. Now was the time, as she had every

intention of making the first boat ride across the lake. Tickets were

thirteen dollars and worth every penny. Enola took snapshots there

and back. She watched two bald eagles soaring in the sky to the

right, watched a large sheet of ice cling to the side of the mountain ahead of her, and watched the smoke disguise the mountain's middle.

It was beautiful. She thought about how rolling fields and dusty Indian towns had turned into this. Northern Montana was a different animal. When she got back to shore, she walked into a small gift shop where she noticed a few souvenirs proudly advertising The Road to The Sun. She asked the store clerk what that meant.

"It's a road that will take you across the entire Glacier National Park." He answered.

"You're kidding." Enola's eyes lit up. "Can I do it on three-fourths of a tank?"

"Absolutely." He answered. "It's a cool road. There are so many areas where you're driving right along the edge with a two or three thousand foot drop off to the side."

"How do I get there?" Enola asked with excitement in her voice.

"Take this road," he pointed on a map. "And go to the stop sign and turn left. Follow that road until you get to the Saint Mary building, and then you'll see the entrance to another part of the park." He smiled at Enola's anxious face. "Just go in."

"Thanks a lot." She smiled at him before hurrying out to her car like she was on a mission.

The winding road was picturesque and breathtaking at every turn and angle. She drove watching for sliding rock, bear, mountain goats, and more eagles, but being careful at the same time to watch the road in front of her. Sometimes she would find herself alone for miles and miles; other times she would be in a caravan of curious on-seekers. She stopped whenever her gut told her to: waterfalls, optimum views of a glacier, and once when the rain came down hard. That's when she decided to pull off the road and just watch the rain. A thirty-minute downpour.

When she came out of the other side of Glacier National Park, she felt accomplished and proud of herself. She saw a sign returning her to 2 West. Quickly, she got on it.

By the last week of July, Enola was still in Montana, so were another fifty-pounds of Asad Harb's explosives.

#

Butte, Montana was only five hours away from Libby, where Enola tossed and turned most of the night. Finally, tired of fighting it, she sat up in the back of her car, which she had parked overnight at The Venture Inn. She looked good for a woman turning fifty-five in one week, but she knew finding a shower had taken top priority in her life, so she made her way to a truck stop up the street on her right, pulled-in and swung a small black backpack over her shoulder containing shampoo, crème rinse, liquid dial soap, and a toothbrush and toothpaste. Twenty minutes later, she was back to smelling like coconut milk and spring-scented soap, and five minutes after that, the nerves in her stomach felt like they were under attack. CHEW.

She stood, watching the television, alongside two male truckers, both tired and old from the road, something she wondered if she'd look soon, if she didn't decide what to do with her life. Her thoughts turned back to the television, as she listened to the news-woman: *Police are on the scene at several locations in Butte, Montana this morning, after they say a forty-one-year-old man called in several bomb threats. The first one was made to Butte Courthouse this morning, where police tell us a recorded message warned that explosives were in the building. The second was made to*

Butte High School, where 1,200 students were promptly evacuated. The bomb squad recovered fifty-pounds of explosives, but are not releasing the exact amounts found in each building. Students have been sent home for the day pending further search efforts. The courthouse has canceled all sessions until further notice. An arrest has been made. We will keep you updated.

"I bet you anything, that's because of O'Neill." The burly trucker with a plaid shirt and white beard said out loud.

"You might be right." Replied the slender build. His face was clean-shaven, but missing several front teeth. "But that O'Neill is a hero, in my fucking opinion." He said it with a tone that didn't want an argument. "He did the world a favor by killing Osama bin Laden."

"Hell, I agree with you Chip, but I'm just worried that ISIS is still holding a grudge against that homegrown hero." The face with the white beard looked concerned.

"Rob ain't scared of no one." Slender rebutted.

"You got that right." The plaid shirt moved as it laughed.

I left wondering who Rob O'Neill was. *Was he the man who killed Osama bin Laden? Was ISIS seeking revenge?* And then, *I'm glad we have men like Rob O'Neill*. She felt a little safer as she thought his name. A real-life hero.

A feeling of calmness stayed with Enola into Idaho, where she stopped at the Moyie River Bridge to snap a few photos. *Beautiful*. She thought. The feeling on her freshly showered skin matched her mood, and the mountains in Sandpoint, teased her sense of time to slow down. First a green-iced-tea at Starbucks, then more shampoo and conditioner from Walmart, and finally, she made her way in an unfamiliar fast-food restaurant, Zips. She had never heard of one before, but wanted a cold drink and some food, so she studied her choices before ordering: *cod basket with fries*. It went down easy, especially their homemade tartar sauce, enough to push her forward.

#

Spokane was dark by the time I arrived. Too dark to see what it looked like, and I was tired anyway, so I pulled off to my right, off 2 West, and into the parking lot of a La Quinta Inn. I shut my eyes, but felt the vibration of my phone beside me.

"Hello." I said, then realizing it was Allie, "Hey sweetie."

"I'm just checking on you to make sure you're safe." She sounded like I sounded so many times with her.

"I am." And then, "Are you and Reese doing okay?" I smiled before adding on what felt natural. "Are you safe?"

"Yes, we're doing great." And then with a hint of regret in her voice, "They found that woman."

"What woman?" *Yellow Bird*, I remembered before she could answer.

"Carla Yellow Bird, the woman who disappeared in North Dakota."

"Is she okay?" I questioned, but could tell by the disappointing tone in Allie's voice, that she wasn't.

"No, they found her body on an Indian reservation. Someone shot and killed her." I knew she was upset at how cruel the world can be. I googled a photo of Carla Yellow Bird, while I listened to her talk about how she hoped the murderer would be found. *She looks a lot like Allie.* I thought. *Young. Beautiful.* And then, *no wonder it's hitting her so hard.*

"I'm sorry Allie." I wanted to say more, wanted to tell her that evil wasn't everywhere, but I knew differently. "I love you so much." I didn't know what else to say.

"Gvgeyui." She said the Cherokee Indian word with deep sincerity, our word, something to hold on to when the rest of the world doesn't make sense.

"Gvgeyui," I answered back, one word, but the three most important words we had. *I love you.* "Lock your doors tonight." I reminded her, my uneasiness and distrust returned at once. I listened to her gentle goodbye. I didn't know how to protect her in a world full of hatred. Deep breath. BITE. I looked at the dark western sky as I thought about Bobby in Detroit and beautiful Yellow Birds, the purple dandelions of the world.

Chapter Nine

Several members of the Usurpers, a street gang, stood outside the

Multnomah County Courthouse, off Fourth Avenue, in Portland.

Enola moved slowly by with her red Hyundai, eyeing the group.

Their faces wore one emotion – anger. The largest man, wore a wife-

beater shirt in the still August air, showing-off his upper arm tattoo,

the outline of a family crest, with a dagger in the background, its

detail revealing a double-edged blade, and the foreground exploded

into a large red letter. Enola drove slowly by, able to make out the letter, a bright red U. She imagined it was the initial for his first name, *perhaps Ulysses*, she thought, finding the name funny, envisioning a tiny newborn being named after the James Joyce novel, 730 pages describing a single day. She laughed, thinking about her college attempt to read the novel, set in Dublin, the main character, someone she could relate to, his mother dead, his father estranged, and in his adult life, he becomes a teacher, whose spouse has an affair, and then in 730 pages, he spends a single day, in his middle-aged life, trying to find peace and serenity. She laughed again, this time at the similarities between herself and the James Joyce character, laughter that suddenly made her feel uneasy, as she noticed the man in the sleeveless shirt staring at her. His eyes looked directly into her blue ones, which were completely unaware that he was a member of the Usurpers, and was surrounded by those just like him, men who sized her up as she drove by. She tried not to look directly into his eyes, but couldn't help it, drawn to the darkness, even though they appeared to be a lighter color. *He's not a purple dandelion.* Enola concluded, before slowly driving by, his lingering stare followed her, sending chills down her spine.

Fifteen minutes later she was exiting her car, after parking it as close as possible to the Burnside Bridge, where she stood with families as they rooted on hundreds of bicyclists participating in the ride over the city's two major bridges: Burnside and Morrison. She still felt the evil stare, and slowly began to piece it together, as she eyed the front page of a newspaper, center-stage in a metal paper box near her. She read the first paragraph without changing her footing:

> Rodney Collinsworth has been charged with murder, after running down a nineteen-year-old with his vehicle, near a shopping plaza last month. Collinsworth a member of the Usurpers, is a well-known white supremacist. Authorities recovered weapons, illegal drugs, and forty-pounds of explosives from his apartment in Portland.

Enola pulled up a photo of the victim, on her phone – *a handsome young black man, his face innocent, his life cut short.* Then more thoughts followed. *The world is full of dividing lines.* She pulled her eyes away from the green metal newspaper box, the keeper of stories filled with hatred and evil. She walked back to her car, deciding she needed to find a place where she could feel safe; she ended up near a window in Café Yumm off Third Street in downtown Portland, a welcomed break. She dug into the bowl of jasmine rice, chili, tomatoes, black olives, and the freshest avocado she had ever tasted. She let the textures mix, let them roll around inside her mouth, and allowed herself to imagine a world where kindness prevailed.

#

Incompetent assholes. That was the thought going through Asad Harb's mind, as he looked over his records: Ten-pounds of explosives recovered at the nightclub in Tampa. Thirty-pounds of explosives recovered from the box-truck in Nice, France. Fifty-pounds of explosives recovered from the courthouse and high school in Butte, Montana. Forty-pounds of explosives recovered from Collinsworth's apartment in Portland, Oregon, and now, as he had recently been informed by one of his sources, twenty-pounds recovered from his dead brother's home. *One-hundred and fifty-pounds recovered by the ATF.* Asad calculated in his head, and then, a thought hit him, *maybe I'm going to have to be the one who steps up the game.*

#

I needed time alone, as ironic as that sounded for someone in my position. I drove seventy miles back into Washington state. I don't know why. I had spent two days in Spokane before going down to Portland, but I wanted more of Washington. My skin yearned for the way it tingled, as I drove through Washington's dips, ravines, mountains, peaks, and valleys. The landscape soothed the flutters inside me. The view of Mount Saint Helen's pulled me forward. I could see her every detail: ravines that curved inward, sharp edges that jutted outward, a blotched painting of ash and rock haphazardly depicted in a random pattern. She looked calm – for now, not like she had when she exploded in anger, the last time, in May 1980, sending water, ash, and rock down the south side, clearing everything in its path for miles. I thought about how a volcano could be put in the same category as animals and humans – each has the ability to explode, and each has the ability to destroy lives. But at the moment, and given the choice, I'd take the volcano. There, I watched the sun disappear, darkness and cold settling around me, my car parked unnoticed, at the base of the 1980 destruction, as a deep-throated whine, mixed with yips, and high-pitched squeals filled the night air that surrounded me. Total darkness. I listened. First a light whimper, then a growl that seemed to snort and playfully pounce

with another. *Coyote?* I questioned. *How many are there?* I couldn't

see ten inches past my hand, but I was certain they were traveling

closer. Snarl. A musical arrangement of howls. I stayed hidden

underneath my only three blankets, wishing I could understand their

language. I couldn't. Instead, I dozed off in respectful reverence,

analyzing the pecking order in my sleep.

I slept for almost six hours, before daylight welcomed me,

and before working my way into a standing position just outside my

car, close enough for safety, in case I still had visitors, but room

enough to brush my teeth using Listerine, and comb out my knotted

hair. I looked up at Mount Saint Helen in the early daylight. She

stood strong; I knew I could too.

After planning my route, I headed toward Tumwater,

Washington where I pulled into the parking lot of a restaurant called

PHO 102. The warmth of broth, rice noodles, sprouts, and chicken

filled an empty spot inside of me. I carefully maneuvered each bite

onto my chopsticks, before texting Allie, and attempting to reach

Mitch on WhatsApp. I missed them both, and I knew that

communication with them, renewed the warmth inside of me – an unspoken agreement between the three of us, that we would always love each other, without judgment, and keep moving forward.

I made Seattle by three in the afternoon. I searched the skyline as I drove in, spotting the Space Needle. I had dreamed of seeing it, and now, I was less than a mile away. I made my way in the traffic and on one-way streets to a parking garage across from the towering icon. I hurried across the road, snapped a few upward photos, and questioned the first people I saw who worked there about a ticket to ride up the elevator. I wanted to soar above Seattle like a bird. The skyline couldn't have been more inviting. My ticket was for seven p.m., enough time for me to walk up and down Broad Street. I looked at the Chihuly glass display, in a nearby gift shop, took in the roses and magnolia that surrounded the sidewalk, watched a large seagull strut across the grass, and took in the smells and sounds of Seattle. It was a beautiful city.

The elevator went up quickly to the observation deck. I walked out 520 feet above the ground, clicked my way around the deck, snapping photos of the tallest building, the Pacific Ocean, Mount Rainier, and Mount Baker. The view left me open-mouthed, as my skin absorbed the sixty-five-degree temperature and powerful smell of salt air. TICKLE. Happy to be alive, I inhaled deeply.

#

By time Enola May made Anacortes, Washington, it was on every radio station. Five people had been shot and killed at the Cascade Mall, about sixty miles north of Seattle, and only seventeen miles from where Enola now stood. Witnesses had seen the man, armed with a rifle and backpack. Four women. One man. Dead. Enola pulled over, putting her hands to her face, wiping tears for people that died senselessly. *Why?* She questioned.

Anacortes, Washington, on Fidalgo Island, was a sleepy town compared to Seattle, yet because of the manhunt that was only thirty-minutes away, nowhere felt safe. Not tonight. Enola ducked into Calico's for a turkey pot pie and raspberry ice tea, explored a few antique shops that were still open, and snapped a few photos of the hanging flower baskets lining the street – anything to get her mind off the victims at the Cascade Mall. *Breathe.* She had to remind herself. She was conscious of the flutter inside her stomach. It felt like giant wings, this time cutting her insides. Feelings of her childhood, of fear, and of uncertainty manifested, and control disappeared. She thought about the feelings she had in her stomach.

Uneasiness. Uncertainty. The gentle nibble became more forceful.

GNAW.

Chapter Ten

I boarded the 8:25 Washington State Ferry in Anacortes to

Vancouver Island, but not before picking up a newspaper, anxious to

read the story about the shooting. *Did they catch the shooter?* I

wondered. I was comforted by the fact that they had – a twenty-year-

old immigrant from Turkey. But, my sadness for the victims and

their families still had me fighting tears. I couldn't understand it. The

article talked about how the man's Twitter account had posted

photos of ISIS leaders Baghdadi and Khamanei. I didn't even know who those men were, but I knew killing people in the name of someone's beliefs was unforgivable. My eyes filled with tears. I lingered over the name of the youngest victim. *Sarai.* Sixteen. Her life just beginning. I thought of Allie. Thought of how fragile life is. I hadn't cursed at the sky in a long time, since my second divorce, but I felt anger as I looked at the sky above, and I continued feeling it until the ferry reached Vancouver Island.

I spent the next several hours ducking in and out of bookstores, antique shops, boutiques, and questioning my faith. I hadn't done that in years, and was slowly coming to the conclusion that I didn't have any. None. Just since leaving Florida, I had seen first-hand, the despair of neighborhoods overrun with drugs, witnessed racism, been forced to acknowledge dividing lines, stood at the foot of buildings that had disappeared with thousands of lives, and had seen eyes the color of evil, those that murder, those that feel no empathy, the psychopaths, the devils on earth.

I tried not to let it break me. Instead, I bit into thick layers of white meaty fish, at the quaint little wooden restaurant, Fish on Fifth, as I sipped tea, studied faces, searched for kindness, and smiled back at people who needed something to believe in. I lingered until the sky in Sidney turned into various shades of pink and purple, before

making my way back to the ferry. There, I let the sound of waves fill

my head, as white caps slammed the sides of the boat, and a gray

whale broke the water's surface twenty-feet out to my left. I smiled.

The next morning, I wiggled down Interstate 5, and then

made a left on 90 East. Cle Elum, Washington was nestled just over

the Cascade Mountain Range, a welcoming town, full of greenery

and pleasant people. I stopped at a Taco Bell, ordered at crunchy

taco, order of nachos, and Orange Cream Pop Freeze, letting the icy

fragments of vanilla and orange tantalize my taste buds. After

enough nourishment to get me going again, I maneuvered my car

through peaks and valleys that dipped into a golden yellow, littered

with wind turbines that sat high and proud, their large white blades

cutting the air, shafts spinning, and kinetic energy being converted

and dispersed. *Why can't people be converted?* And then, *can evil be*

metamorphosized to good? I continued to drive, processing the

question.

By nightfall, I had made it to La Grande, where I pulled over

in time to have a phone conversation with Allie, undistracted,

listening to her idea about meeting up, *maybe Yellowstone National*

Park, I listened passionately. The thought made me excited. I knew she had left Arizona, and was traveling in Colorado, exploring, playing with the idea of seeing Wyoming, but I never thought about the distance between us, never calculated the possibility of getting to spend time with Allie and Reese.

"I can't wait to see you Mom." She paused. "I'm thinking we could meet somewhere in Wyoming." She added. "To celebrate your birthday."

"I'm so excited Allie." It was an understatement. "I wasn't thinking about my birthday." It was a partial truth. I knew I was a few days away from officially being fifty-five. I guess what I didn't know was where I would be on my birthday, the sixth of August. Now, I had a goal – to be near Allie.

"Okay. Gvgeyui," she said. I teared up when she said it. "We'll firm up our meeting spot as we both get closer."

"Gvgeyui." I answered back before agreeing.

#

Thursday afternoon, Enola slowed, stopping at Craters of the Moon, pulled-in by the national park's promise of seeing lava rock. A young attendant handed her a brochure on the way in. Enola pulled to a stop, glancing, reading about Snake River, the eruption of

underground volcanoes, and the aftermath, a world of cinder cone,

splatter lava, fissures, and rifts. She spent a couple of hours in the

park, her eyes soaking in the foreign landscape, her hands touching

textures that made her feel like she was walking on the moon. For a

while, she felt lost in a different world, a feeling that became funny

to her, when she pulled into Arco, Idaho later that evening, seeking

refuge in the corner of The Lost River Motel parking lot. It sat upon

a hill across from Pickle's Place, a mom and pop restaurant that

specialized in hamburgers, fries, onion rings, and clam chowder.

Perfect. She thought. *I'll grab a bowl of clam chowder and a small*

order of onion rings from Pickle's Place and head across the street

to my dark retreat.

The lights around the top of the motel were in a pattern of

green, yellow, orange, and purple, and at ground level, cute

walkways were bordered by small lights and sculptured metal

dragonflies. Enola May watched them change from blue, to pink, to

yellow, and finally to green, a cycle that repeated itself, while she

drank down the last of her clam chowder and ate her final onion ring,

all before dosing off to sleep.

When she opened her eyes, daylight had stilled the alternating colors. The lights along the roof of the motel had been turned off. *Time to go.* She concluded, before swabbing her face with a body wipe, before pulling her hair back into a clip, before crawling into the driver's seat, and before mapping out her route, all the while, keeping in mind that she would be meeting Allie somewhere in Wyoming, tomorrow.

Enola hadn't driven very long, before she stopped at a rest area just east of Arco, where she stood reading a sign about how Arco was a test site for atomic bombs in 1945. *My mother's birth year.* She remembered. Then, the fact that she found most ironic, she noticed she was standing in the exact location once used for atomic bomb testing. *How fitting.* Enola grinned, as she knew she was named after the plane that had dropped the first atomic bomb. *The Enola Gay.* She found the similarities baffling. *Same year my mother was born.* And then, *atomic bombs.* And, an added thought, *coming across all this one day before my birthday.* She laughed out loud, knowing no matter how much she didn't want to believe in God, that something was out there. *Thanks, mom.* She knew the universe had a good sense of humor. Refreshed and hungry, she made her way to

Idaho Falls, where she stopped at a Burger King on West Broadway,

and ordered an unsweet tea and Whopper Jr. with cheese. Using her

phone, she connected to the internet and emailed Mitch, even though

her last two emails remained unanswered; then, she sent Allie a

message stating her location. An hour passed, before Allie

responded, and several messages were exchanged before agreeing on

a time and place. Late tomorrow. Cody, Wyoming. Walmart parking

lot. Enola's birthday.

Chapter Eleven

It was almost midnight when I heard her knock at my back window.

I sat up quickly, excited at the fact that her voice was only inches

from me. I opened my car door to the mild fifty-degree temperature,

Allie's smile, a beat-up 2002 Chevy Tahoe, two anxious dogs that I

had never met – the first, a black lab and wolf mix, and the second, a

black and white pit bull mix – and Reese, the young man of only

twenty-three that my daughter loved.

"I missed you," I said, hugging her the entire time. "Where the heck did two dogs come from?" I laughed, wondering how they managed living and traveling in a Chevy Tahoe with two large dogs.

"Happy Birthday Mom." She said studying my expression. "I knew you'd be shocked." She smiled, her passion toward animals showing in the glow on her face. "We found Shiloh in the Arizona desert; someone dumped her there." I thought of Dacey Fears, the man who abandoned my childhood German shepherd, his cruelty toward animals, and toward people, for that matter. "And, Zeus, was cast aside when his owners had a baby; they were going to have him put down." She had the same look on her face as I did on mine. *People are cruel.*

"You've always been so passionate and loving," I said. Then I quickly turned to give Reese a hug who was standing there the entire time, trying to control Shiloh and Zeus who were anxious to jump on me.

The three of us walked the dogs around the Walmart lot for almost an hour, my first hour of being fifty-five years old. Allie and Reese talked about Arizona, talked about how much they loved traveling, and talked about how excited they were to go to

Yellowstone National Park. It was almost three in the morning,

before we each bedded down in our own cars for a few hours, before

heading into Walmart at first light, and before buying three-days-

worth of groceries for the park. Marshmallows, chocolate bars,

graham crackers, hamburgers, pepper jack cheese, onion, hamburger

buns, corn on the cob, beef sausages paired with hotdog buns, three

thin steaks, charcoal, and lots of bottled water. We managed to fit all

of it into my front passenger seat and floor, of course Allie and

Reese grabbed a large bag of Purina One Smart Blend. All set.

We entered the park around ten a.m., by time we each filled

up our tanks with gas and made it to the east side entrance of

Yellowstone. The mountains were a challenge for any car, but Allie

and Reese's Tahoe kept pace with my Hyundai as I glided around

curves, up and down mountainous areas, and dipped into valleys that

looked like postcards. Osprey swarmed over treetops that reached

the sky. We stopped at Lake Butte Overlook which nestled against

Yellowstone Lake. I was the first to spot a buffalo off in the

distance. Even standing so far away, he looked nearly as big as my

Hyundai. We walked to the edge of Yellowstone Lake where Shiloh

quickly jumped in the water, and Zeus followed suit after he made sure Shiloh appeared to be okay. Hesitant. Reese threw a stick out to meet Shiloh, which she rescued with her teeth before swimming back to shore. The weather and bright blue sky called us forward, so we made our way to West Thumb where we stood in awe over a geyser. Throughout the next hour, we saw geysers that ranged from colors of dark brown to bright blue. At one point a mule deer went right in front of my car as we carefully traveled toward Shoshone Lake. We stopped at a pull-off where a black circular strip of pavement was obscured from any travelers. Reese made a fire in a portable grill which they carried along with them, and I pulled the three steaks from the small ice chest in my front passenger seat, and prepped them for the grill that was almost ready, while Allie pulled off the corn husks exposing three separate ears of corn on the cob.

The day and night couldn't have been more perfect. I watched the stars move above my head as I crawled under my three blankets in the back of my car, all the while trying to protect myself from temperatures that had dropped to the mid-forties. I could hear the wind through the one-inch openings at the top of each window, but I wanted to feel the coldness that surrounded me. Besides, I felt warm inside knowing Allie was five feet away in her vehicle snuggling with Reese, two happily panting dogs sleeping at their

feet. I allowed myself to feel the calmness inside of me. No flutter.

STILL. Soothed by the wind and knowledge that my daughter was

near.

We made it to Old Faithful by two the next afternoon, but not

before rounding a corner and coming upon a herd of buffalo. They

blocked the road, some bigger than my car. We waited. Admiring

and carrying on a conversation car to car by phone. When they

cleared, we continued, coming upon an enormous bull elk off to the

right. He was nestled under a tree, his head adorned with a massive

set of antlers, and his body, at least 700 hundred pounds, had been

lowered into a sitting position, partially hidden in a self-made hole,

giving him the comfortable task of keeping look-out. I wondered if

he was guarding his family, nearby, a faithful servant. I pondered my

perception, as we wiggled our way to Old Faithful, the famous

geyser located in Yellowstone. *Faithful.* Analyzing the name, I

found it ironic that nature is capable of earning titles that few people

obtain. We settled into observatory mode, watching the forceful

ejection of steam and water, a rare exhibition, in a class of its own,

something that should be appreciated, and protected; otherwise, like a relationship, it will become dormant, and lifeless. I watched the hot water shoot up in the air a good seventy-five feet. I grabbed Allie's hand as the three of us sat together. She felt warm and alive, and her eyes were soaking in the good of the world. I wished she only saw good, but I knew I couldn't protect her from the evil that was out there. I looked in her chocolate eyes. She was a good person – a purple dandelion.

"I love you." It was the fifth or sixth time I had said it since morning.

"I love you too Mom." She squeezed my hand back.

Afterward, we drove to Mammoth Hot Springs, stopping when we spotted two bighorn sheep off in a field of yellow grass and wildflowers. I started to tear up when I looked at Allie and Reese standing beside me, knowing that in just a few days we would have to part. Our paths weren't meant to be one. They had to go their own way in life. I knew I could be a part of it at times, but only now and then, for the most part I needed to let them find their own way. I remembered as I put my arm around her and fought back tears, that I had to find my own way too.

"Thanks for bringing us here," Allie said. I knew she was referring to the admission and to the groceries we had been living on.

"You're welcome," I said honestly. And then, "We can't replace this time." She knew what I meant. I could tell there was still a part of her that missed being a child and having all my attention, especially after Mitch left home at eighteen, left to find his own path. That's the moment when being the last child in the household has its advantages. The focus was all on her – on us. Still, I wondered if Mitch remembered his time before her, time that was just his – my first child, my son, the first person I would ever love unconditionally. Now, I felt he was in another world, at times, unavailable, closed off, and dormant like a geyser, whose insides had been littered with foreign objects, causing it to shut down.

My thoughts stayed with me, even as we stopped to hike at Mammoth Hot Springs, a mixture of everything great about Yellowstone. It towered in a breathtaking landscape above the roadway. Wooden paths maneuvered their way up to the top of geysers and hot springs, where we made our way by foot, snapping photos of gold, yellow, and white that had the appearance of hardened snow.

By time we hiked back to our vehicles, we were tired and hungry, so we made our way to Canyon Village to spend the night in a campground, where volunteering to cook, I quickly let the scent of sausages, onion, corn on the cob and baked beans fill the air around our campsite, and fill the empty spaces in our stomachs. We sat around the campfire, with Zeus and Shiloh, their bellies full of Purina One, and the sky full of endless stars.

The next morning, after two hours of laundry and showers, we made our way to the west entrance of Yellowstone, where we exited, taking memories with us. We agreed to travel together for a few more days, spilling over into Montana shortly after leaving Yellowstone, and then pouring into Idaho within an hour's drive. Allie followed my lead, pulling into a campground called The Wild Rose, cradled in a valley, between a mountain of gold and a lake that looked painted blue, appearing too perfect to be real. Twenty-seven dollars later we had a spot to park our vehicles. Shiloh and Zeus were anxious to get out of the Tahoe, making their way to a small stream that ran behind our camp spot, while Reese started a grill. He cooked hamburgers with pepper jack cheese, a perfect aroma to complement the mountain air. Afterward, we walked to the lake and threw three lines in the water. Reese had been wanting to fish since Yellowstone, but we had been too busy hiking and exploring. Here we were able to take some time to do nothing but fish. I held a pole in my hands that he had handed me. I felt something tug at my line, so gently I reeled in, only to feel it let go. *Let go.* I thought to myself. *It's time to let go.* But parting was something neither one of us wanted to do. Two more nights, we all agreed, so we left The Wild Rose in Idaho by ten a.m., making it to Twin Falls in enough time for me to pick up a few things at a grocery store, and enough time for Allie and Reese to sell some of Allie's handmade wire-wrapped pendants and Reese's hand-carved pipes, hidden talents they both had, to help them drum up gas and food money when needed. We met up in time to secure a safe camping spot, overlooking the Perrine Bridge, had pizza we ordered from a nearby Pizza Hut, and spent the evening in deep conversation – politics, religion, crime, and even aliens.

Morning came early, and soon we were carving our way through mountains, past small waterfalls that dripped onto the road, and entering Shoshone Falls Park. Bright green grass and plastic picnic tables sat steadily on rolling hills, where we constructed turkey and pepper jack sandwiches and quickly devoured them, before grabbing a couple of water bottles, and hiking closer to the falls, that roared in the early afternoon silence. Allie pulled a tiny box from her pocket and handed it to me. I looked at her, admiring her smile and ingenuity, before opening the box, carefully, being cautious not to spill the contents into the rushing water, that flowed nearby. Inside was a bright pink heart, that she had put on a silver chain. I anxiously read the engraving: Gvgeyui Forever. I started to cry as she smiled at me.

"I love you so much Mom. It's your birthday present." She hugged me, then, "I'm sorry it's a few days late."

"It's beautiful Allie." I smiled at her. "I love you." Wiping tears from my eyes, and looking into her brown ones, the same ones her father used to love me with, I said the word. "Gvgeyui," I went in for a hug. "This means so much to me." I caught a glimpse of Reese looking at us. It was admiration, as he stepped back trying to give us a moment, but I reached for his arm pulling him closer, his other arm holding two leashes, both with dogs that were anxious to explore. He didn't resist; instead, he hugged us both. I would always love Allie, and I would always love whomever she chose to love. That was a gift that all parents should give their children – a gift I wish I had received from Melantha, and a gift I would give to Mitch, if he'd let me be part of his life.

But, for now, the universe gave me what it could.

Chapter Twelve

Fifteen young men, hands bound, and forced to their knees, faced their graves. Within moments, a bullet sent fragmented pieces of each man's skull into the Syrian dirt. Asad Harb smiled as he watched the report on the news from his Detroit home. *I'm glad they were executed.* He thought. *Like my brother.* He shook his head at their arrogance. *Traitors. Exposing the ISIS headquarters in Qaim.* He stood proud, in his father's memory, and in light of the successful events that had occurred over the last week. *My explosives are making headlines.* He proudly thought, knowing that the recent

three-day binge, triggering terror in New Jersey and New York, were

from *his* explosives. *Finally, sixty-pounds of explosives put to good*

use. The first twenty – a pipe bomb in Seaside. BOOM. The second

twenty – reconfigured into a cooker-bomb in Manhattan. SPLAT.

And the third twenty – planted in the train station in Elizabeth.

SCREAM. *Too bad no one was killed.* A slight frown. *Only injuries.*

He took a deep breath. *Maybe next time.*

#

A small church painted white with three windows faced the two-lane

road, its surface visited by scrub brush and tumbleweeds. The only

other business, a store that appeared empty, appropriately titled A to

Z, stood in the belly of Wells, Nevada. There, Enola was reminded

she was alone, so she continued to drive, making her way to West

Wendover, while Allie, her free-spirited daughter, made her way to

the coast of California with Reese and their two rescued dogs.

Casinos, their signs on fire with shades of red, blue, green,

and yellow neon, welcomed her. The Rainbow Casino's lights

screamed the loudest, inviting her inside for a hamburger and soda

and a chance to play the penny slot machines. She gambled twenty-

five cents with the push of each button, until employees at The
Rainbow quickly ran from room to room, making sure that all guests
had heard the most recent announcement: *Attention patrons, at this
time we would like you to exit as quickly as possible.* Enola looked
up, a twenty-four-dollar slot voucher lying near her right hand, the
one that had been pushing the black button on *The Wizard of Oz*,
now stilled, as her eyes caught a glimpse of uniformed officers
heading in her direction. She quickly pressed the cash-out button,
retrieved another white-slip of paper, adding two dollars and thirteen
cents to her win total, and headed toward the exit, other patrons
scurried in front and behind her. She questioned the hurry, but didn't
stop to ask; instead, the question disappeared as she saw two men in
EOD suits, Explosive Ordnance Disposal. *Bomb.* She thought, trying
not to panic, but stealing another glance of the men in full body
armor. She wasn't allowed to go to her car, a safety precaution;
instead, officers directed patrons off property, and away from the
parking lot. She stood in the darkness for hours, watching lights, but
not the ones on the casino, no, these were atop West Wendover
police cars. Her first thought was to call Allie, but she didn't want to
worry her, so she simply stood, taking in the chatter between

patrons. It was almost midnight by the time the parking lot and casino entrances were reopened. Enola went in, long enough to cash out her slips from the slot machines. Twenty-six dollars and thirteen cents.

#

Asad Harb was pissed. *Why did I believe things were finally going to go right?* He questioned himself. First of all, the fifty-pounds of explosives were supposed to make it to Las Vegas, Nevada, not West Wendover. Secondly, they were supposed to spill blood, not become another entry on ATF's recovery log. *Dammit.* He silently muttered. *I guess that's what happens when you send a chronic gambler to do a man's job.* Still, he had hope that things would go better in Salt Lake City. Success in Salt Lake would honor his father's memory, would honor his father's Islamic theology, and would promote peace, a belief his father had. *Asad, the world will know peace when all Jews have been obliterated.* He remembered his father's words, said many times, passionate, and not up for argument. That's why The Jewish Community Center in Utah was an important target, one that Asad didn't want the ATF to add to their recovery log – another forty-pounds.

#

Enola woke after five hours of sleep, and drove until roads flattened and the colorless median expanded into an endless patch of white. The Morton Salt Factory stood boldly off to her right. *Peculiar.* She thought as she kept driving. *It that how Salt Lake got its name?* She wondered, then pulled over to google it on her phone. *The numerous rivers don't have an outlet.* She gathered. *That's why there's so much salt in the area.* She watched the white patches widen, then lessen, as she got closer to downtown. There, the sky was filled with tall office buildings, a delicate architectural lace of concrete and block, an array of decorated churches, and a capital building that proudly overlooked the city. Enola wondered how a city with such extravagant buildings could turn such a blind eye to the overabundance of homeless people, shopping carts being pushed to-and-fro, lines of handwash hanging from trees, blankets that housed homeless mothers and children, and parks that served as gathering spots for men to congregate and share stories of death and hopelessness. Salt Lake was a mixture of riches and rags, of prosperity and poverty, of hope and despair. She closed her eyes, trying to process both ends of the spectrum, before her silence was interrupted. BOOM. The sound was deafening. At first, Enola looked out to her driver's side window, toward Pioneer Park. Faces that had been covered with blankets, stirred, sitting upright, searching the skyline in the direction of Enola's passenger window.

Black smoke filled the sky. *Fire?* Enola questioned. *An explosion?* She replayed the sound. Firetrucks raced by stunned faces. Traffic came to a halt, limiting Enola's options. She felt in the way, even though she had pulled off the road as much as possible. Siren after siren passed her.

It wasn't until three in the afternoon before the streets began to clear. Enola was hungry, realizing she hadn't eaten all day; although, food seemed to be too self-serving at the moment. Still, there was nothing she could do, except follow the other cars, and move away from the sound that had rocked Salt Lake. She drove until the largest part of the city was behind her, finally pulling over at a Chipotle, where she purchased a to-go bowl of brown rice, chicken, and peppers, before settling on the coffee shop next door for seating and a drink with coconut milk. Sitting at the window inside, she watched people as she ate her meal and drank down the coconut milk with a hint of caramel and decaf coffee. She listened as two off-duty police officers talked about the explosion, pulling bits and pieces together: a man carrying explosives, prematurely went off, killing the bomber, blew up three unoccupied cars and the front windows of the Jewish Community Center. She could tell by the way they were talking that no other human life was taken, except for the man with the explosives. It was too coincidental – a nightclub, a courthouse, schools, casinos, and a community center. She wondered how many times she had come close to dying, without her knowledge, how many bombs ticked near her, how many loaded guns were tucked into the waistband of a stranger, and how many psychopaths had glanced in her direction – considering her a possible target. Stopping her thoughts, she texted Allie: *I miss you. I love you with all my heart. Where are you?* Allie texted back within just a few minutes: *We're in Yreka, California. I miss you too, Mom. What's your next stop? Are you safe?* She didn't want to tell her about the casino evacuation or the explosion that had just occurred in Salt Lake. Instead, she answered: *Tomorrow I'm going to Arches National Park. I'll take photos. Travel carefully. Gvgeyui.* Then Enola waited for the word she needed before leaving with a full belly and finding a place to sleep: *Gvgeyui.*

#

Mother of All Bombs. The thought occurred to me, as soon as I entered Arches National Park, where I faced an artistic arrangement of boulders and twisted rock, towering spirals, and massive balls the size of mansions, formed from a mixture of red rock and clay. Each unique piece looked like it was part of a majestic, but eerie-stage for the end of the world. *How ironic*, I thought, once again, wondering if Melantha had something to do with what seemed like another sign from the universe. *M-O-A-B*. I analyzed each letter of the city's name, smiling at the humor, as I continued to drive slowly, taking in the delicate arches that dripped beneath an endless sky. Pulling off to the side of the road, I walked between slabs of earth that sprouted upward, infinitely strong, real, and everlasting. I bent over, picking up a quarter-size piece of red clay, rolling it between my fingers, and thinking about a documentary I had watched years back, about the Moab-bomb, recalling how U.S. Military personnel polished it, like a brand-new car, only this one was over 20,000 pounds and about thirty feet long. The day they decided to test it, I nervously watched the Florida sky, searching for the mushroom-shaped cloud of smoke that people near the city of Pensacola reported, hoping the effects didn't expand past the test site of the Eglin Airforce base. Mitch was thirteen, at the time, talking about Saddam Hussein in school. Allie was only seven, unaware that the United States was getting ready to initiate war on Iraq, in order to destroy Hussein's weapons of mass destruction that could be used against the United States. *I hope you know what you're doing President Bush.* I remembered saying to myself, my kids too young to understand how temporary existence can be. Overcome with the fragility found in life, I made my way back to my car and ventured into downtown Moab. I settled on Zax, a small corner restaurant off South Main. Sitting down at a table for two, but ignoring the chair on the other side, as I ordered a slice of pepperoni pizza and a salad. The air was beginning to feel like fall, even in the daylight hours. September was only a few days away.

Chapter Thirteen

A man wore a pair of bright yellow overalls. Underneath he wore a
black long-sleeved shirt, which freakishly hugged his arms, one of
which slanted slightly upward, holding an arrangement of helium-
filled balloons: one yellow, one white, one red, and one orange. The
stranger's face was painted a chalky white, and displayed an upper
lip, stained the color of blood-red, one that remained steady, even
when he turned his head. The boys, twelve and thirteen, first noticed
him when they realized they were the last two standing at the corner
of Second and Maple. Everyone else had gone. At first, they thought

about laughing at the full-grown man dressed as a clown, but became

frightened when the bright red hair followed them, even when the

young boys picked up pace. Running within close proximity to

where he was standing, was the only option they had, to make it to

the Mesa Park Apartments, the only sign of life, and the spot where

both boys lived, Zack on the first floor, and Brian on the second.

Without breathing, so it seemed, they ran, their feet hardly touching

the ground, knuckles clenched, ready to swing, if needed.

Enola's red Hyundai passed the boys, their bodies a blur in

her rearview. *What kind of parents let their kids run around this*

late? She questioned, after swerving into the other lane. She never

noticed the clown.

Five minutes later, she pulled over, to gain her composure, at

the McDonalds off Main in Cortez, and called Dixie. An overdue

call. She hadn't talked to her life-long friend in a while.

"Hey, what are you doing?" Enola asked into the phone.

"Living the life," Dixie answered with a southern smile on

her face.

"How's thirty-five years of marriage?" Enola asked,

remembering the woman she considered her sister, had recently celebrated another year of marriage, while she was somewhere between Salt Lake and Moab.

"We went to dinner at Outback." She said. "I still love him." She laughed, an obvious fact, by the way they still looked at each other. "Where are you Sis?"

"I'm in Cortez, Colorado," Enola answered. They talked for about thirty minutes, long enough to catch up on both ends, minus explosions and violence, which Enola decided wasn't necessary to add to the conversation. Finally, Enola realized she was exhausted, and ended the call, after a few more generalizations, about the effects of global warming and the cause of higher gasoline prices. "Love you Dix."

"I love you too Nola." And then, "Be careful."

Being careful was something she always thought about. She knew her limits, so she decided to stay put in the McDonald's lot. After using the restroom and grabbing a burger, Enola stretched out in the back of her car, on her futon mattress, where she finally fell asleep, until the first sign of daylight and a woman's scream woke her. She sat up, discreetly looking out her windows, catching a glimpse of a man dressed in a clown suit, his silhouette pacing around the front of the fast-food restaurant in the early morning fog.

Before Enola could decipher what action to take, she watched two

Montezuma county black and white patrol cars pull into the parking

lot, with their headlights on high beam, all four facing the red-hair,

that had taken on a neon glow.

"Sir, I need you to put your hands over your head." One of

the officers shouted, using his vehicular public address system, as he

remained crouched behind his open driver's door. I watched, careful

not to move, or become a distraction. Both officers had guns drawn,

and pointed directly at the clown, who remained slightly

camouflaged by the early morning Colorado haze. "Do it now." The

officer belted.

My blue eyes watched the black sleeved shirt raise hands into

the air, one hand releasing a bundle of helium-filled balloons. I

watched the fog devour a yellow dot, an orange, and a red. The

fourth balloon, a match with the man's face, blended into the sky,

before the long simple string that had been bound to it, left the

clown's hand. It wasn't until the balloons left my obstructed vision,

that I noticed the clown's pair of yellow overalls. Bright yellow, like

the man I met at Motor City Soul Food in Detroit. Only this time, the yellow was carelessly splattered with dark red, the color matching

the clown's red-stoic lips.

#

It was the same look that matched Asad Harb's expression. He

remained calm, silent, and serious as he listened to the voice on the

other end of his cell phone. It was not the call he wanted to receive,

but he managed to control his emotions, keeping his thoughts and

plans to himself. *It's time.* That was his only thought after hanging

up, and after hearing about the failed bombing in Salt Lake City,

Utah. He knew the explosives had prematurely detonated, before the

bomber could enter the Jewish Community Center. *It's time.* The

same thought repeated.

#

Enola thought about the young boy who had been lured into a

wooded area in Colorado, as she drove the twisting, turning, up-

down roads, throughout Mesa Verde National Park, where she

slowed for a gray wolf that ran in front of her car, inhaled large

gulps of air at altitudes over 9000 feet above sea level, and took in

the magic of solid rock, majestic mountains, and large pine trees. *He*

was only ten years old. She thought, before parking near a sign marked Cliff Palace. *Lured away from his early morning school bus stop.* The details were in her mind. She wanted to reassure his mother that it wasn't her fault. But, once again she felt helpless. *I'm sorry.* She said the words to the air, as she grabbed a bottle of water and started down the path, where she waited for the park ranger on duty to open the locked gate, leading further down and around dangerous curves, toward the cliff dwellings. Walking carefully, and placing each step solidly, she reached the cliff dwellings just as the sun reached three p.m. The dwellings towered from the base of the mountain to the top, their placement hidden below any on-lookers that stood in the parking lot above. Rock and mortar stood before her, formed into a childlike town of playhouses. Enola looked at the windows and doors, still formed in the dwellings, thought about the Pueblo Indians that had lived there over 800 years ago, as she listened to the park ranger talk about how the Indians would travel to the springs below for water each day, how they raised turkeys for food, and how they used the feathers of those same turkeys as down in their blankets. *For the Indians, a long life meant living to forty.* Enola recalled the park ranger stating that fact, as she carefully climbed the ladder back to the surface. Her thoughts returned to the ten-year-old. She was glad the sadistic clown had been taken into custody, but she was saddened by the life lost. Unfair. She didn't understand why someone would ever harm a child. There were no words. She rode in silence, windows down, letting the cool September air invade her thoughts, as she continued to do the only thing that brought her comfort – drive.

#

The mountain just before Durango was enclosed in a dark gray cloud. Rain. Still, I drove, my forward motion urging the sun to shine. The mountain erupted like a volcano in front of me, as a rainbow seemed to sprout from its insides. I smiled, knowing that life was made of magic moments. Sometimes. Although news radio had reported two more clown sightings, each in different states, but no other attacks.

Nini's Restaurant was a cute little Mexican place off Main, where I sat long enough for a burrito and ice tea, before catching up on needed sleep in the parking lot of the Durango Lodge, a dark corner, where I focused on the flutter inside my gut, the first one I had felt in a couple of days. I placed my hand on the spot where it seemed to be most active. I closed my eyes, trying to see my future, craving dusty towns, and far-away places.

Morning, turned my desires to reality. Farmington, New Mexico, was the poster child for a dusty town, and I imagined that it was the combination of both a small community and the September air, that was affecting my thoughts and taste buds. Hungering for more Mexican, I stopped at La Casita and ordered their version of an enchilada and tamale, both of which were excellent, before I continued driving, about an hour and fifteen more minutes, through rolling hills, freckled with scrub vegetation, and an occasional desert mule deer. I reached the Four Corners Monument by one in the afternoon. A man watched me standing with one foot on Arizona and one on Utah, before offering to take my photo. I agreed, handing him my camera phone, and bending all the way over, stretching my left hand into Colorado and my right into New Mexico. *All four states at one time.* I smiled at the thought, and told the man thank-you, before collecting my phone back that he had used to snap two photos.

Four states. I reminded myself. *Four directions to travel.* Before deciding to make a full circle back to Durango, and through to Pagosa Springs, where I shut off my engine in the corner of a

Walmart lot. A full day of exploring and driving, made me too tired

to do anything, except pick up when Allie called.

"Hi Mom. How was your day?" Allie asked.

"Good, I miss you," I replied. "Are you still in California?"

"No, we made our way to Oregon." Allie sounded excited.

"Reese is selling a bunch of his hand-carved pipes to a store in

Medford." She caught her breath. "We're going to stay in Oregon for

a while, so we can make some money." She informed me. "And,

there's a shop next door that might buy some of my wire-wrap

pendants." I could hear her smile.

"That's great." I was glad to hear they were surviving.

"I love you mom." She sighed into the phone. "We're pulling

up to our camp spot for the night. She was concentrating I could tell.

"I'll talk to you soon."

"Okay, Allie," I responded. "I love you."

#

Enola walked down a street in Colorado Springs, not knowing that

ten and a half months earlier, a man had taken the life of a police

officer and two innocent civilians, as he barricaded himself into the

planned parenthood clinic, a mile from the spot where she was now getting her hair dyed a new shade of dark mocha, a color that highlighted her creamy complexion and bright blue eyes. Exiting, she felt alive, head tilted upward, eyeing several hot air balloons in the fall sky. The first, shaped like a large yellow and black bumblebee, a second containing all the colors of a rainbow, and both making her thirst for a good museum and priceless art. *Santa Fe.* She thought. With a new look and a new attitude, Enola made her way back to her car, and set course to Santa Fe, stopping at Pino's Flea Market, in Las Vegas, New Mexico an hour and fifteen minutes into her drive, and smirking at the discovery that there was another Las Vegas besides the one in Nevada. She browsed through old dishes and discarded knick-knacks, some reminding her of her life when the kids were small, before downsizing, and before hitting the road for what had now been over three months. She texted Allie: *I'm headed to Santa Fe. I love you.* And then, Mitch: *I miss hearing from you. I'm in Las Vegas, New Mexico right now. Can you imagine? I love you Mitch.* Within minutes, she received texts back from both, brightening her day even more. *I love you too Mom. We're still in Medford. Be careful.* And then: *That's funny Ma. I love you.* They were all she had.

Chapter Fourteen

Asad Harb inventoried the explosives he had kept for himself in

Vinny's Self-Storage off Mechanic Street, a hole-in-the-wall

business, most of the units empty or abandoned. He smiled. *Four-*

hundred pounds of explosives. He assured himself, before pulling on

the lock twice and walking away empty-handed. His next thought

came as he shut the door of his 2016 Samand Soren. *A few more*

weeks. Then, *first, I want to see what happens with the remaining*

230 pounds I have out there. He smiled again, thinking of the

Northwest Arkansas Business Women's Conference in Little Rock.

#

A quaint adobe building, that matched the surrounding landscape in

Santa Fe, served as the Georgia O'Keeffe Museum. Enola was

anxious to get inside, but noticed her phone ringing as she parked, an

unfamiliar area code registered on her cell, 518. She swiped right,

answering the call, just as she noticed the location in small print.

New York.

"Ma, I can't talk long." It was Mitch's voice. He sounded

rushed. "I'm leaving for a while." He paused, catching his breath.

"I've taken a job with an oil tanker shipping company."

"Mitch, you're not in Arkansas any longer?" She tried not to

show her disappointment, realizing another trip through Arkansas

would be pointless, and that seeing her son wasn't going to happen

before returning to Florida. "How long will you be gone?"

"At least a year." The information came without emotion.

"I'm getting ready to board now." He released a tidbit. "I'm in New

York." A little more, even though she had gathered that from her cell

phone. Still, Enola had no idea what company he had taken a job with, what destination they were headed to, or if her son would be able to communicate with her from sea.

"Mitch?" Enola was lost for words, Arkansas Zoo seemed like yesterday, his crooked smile still in her memory.

"Ma, I'm sorry. I have to go." She could hear his name being called in the background. "I love you." The sound of a busy seaport filled her head.

"Mitch, I love you so much." She could feel her insides being ripped. TEAR.

"I love you too Ma." He was trying to stay focused. "Keep the same phone number, and I'll try to keep in touch." Then he added, "Please let Allie know that I love her." He hung up the phone, without releasing details, no company, no destination, and a time period that seemed vague. He was gone before Enola could say everything she wanted to say. *I've always loved you Mitch. You can accomplish everything you want in life.* And one last thought. *Don't forget the people who love you.*

Her cell phone remained up to her ear, even though the call had ended. Over. He was gone. She sat in stunned silence, unaware that her eyes were already spilling with emotion. Georgia O'Keeffe would have to wait. Instead, her teary eyes concentrated on the

largest building in the center of Santa Fe – The Cathedral Basilica of

Saint Francis. Bells tolled. *A sign?* She questioned, before making

herself exit the car, and walk around the right side of the church,

passing an open doorway, and glaring in with puffy eyes.

"You can come in if you want." A name-tag with Pacheco

looked at her.

"No, thanks…I don't want to interrupt the service." Enola

answered.

"You know. I was recently in a bad car accident." Pacheco

said. "I was in a coma for a while." He looked into her eyes. "I

shouldn't be here." He continued. "Sometimes God works in

mysterious ways." He smiled. "At least walk around the corner to

the Prayer Garden."

"Thanks," Enola responded in a polite tone. "I'm glad you're

doing better." And, then feeling as if it wouldn't hurt, "I'll go look at

it."

A path led into a well-manicured garden of roses bushes and

walnut trees. Enola sat down on a vacant bench, across from a

bronze statue, a replica of Jesus, sun shining off his sculptured bronze skin, the detailed anatomy revealed muscles that had been shaped by expert artistry. She looked around, noticing no one was in The Prayer Garden except her. She walked closer to the bronze statue, placing the insides of her hands together, and closing her eyes. *Please take care of Mitch and Allie.* Then without uttering another word, she turned slowly, her back to the tomb, and began to walk away. Simultaneously, and once again, the bells in The Cathedral Basilica of Saint Francis tolled. Ding. Dong. Ding. Dong. Ding. Dong.

#

The Bomb Squad Task Force responded to an emergency call from Hammons' Convention Center today, just outside of Little Rock, following routine review of their weekend security footage. Daryl Owens, a security guard at the center, is being hailed as a hero for his quick actions, as well as several bomb-sniffing dogs that spent more than an hour locating the explosives. It was a lucky day for almost fourteen-hundred people, most of them women, as they were promptly evacuated from the building, and one-hundred pounds of explosives were recovered. The news report blared across Asad's living room. This time he picked up the phone.

#

I waited until Friday before I went to the Georgia O'Keeffe

Museum. Studying the colors and shapes she used in each of her

paintings, I walked slowly from room to room, listening to a video

about her life, and tossing over in my head the time period that she

lived, her age when she died, and the strength and courage that were

surely part of her. *Ninety-eight years old.* I thought. *Born thirteen*

years before the nineteenth century ended. I imagined the world

when and where she was born: one of isolation, vast farmland, and

cold Wisconsin winters, while being one of seven siblings.

Nonetheless, she exploded in color, like her paintings, graduating

high school in Virginia, teaching in Texas, studying art in Chicago

and New York, and falling in love with New Mexico's rosy-orange

painted deserts, mesas, and high peaks. *She noticed every curve and*

every color. It was an observation that I gathered, as I stared at her

work: large white flowers jumped from the canvas, valleys of

orange, green, and tan melted together, blue skies became one with

the New Mexico desert, tall buildings towered into the sky, a

representation she painted from her time in New York, and orange

and black circles flirted with curvy blue lines. My favorite, a painting where orange, yellow, lavender, and white swirled over the canvas in delicate motions, made the canvas appear as if it were on fire. I left the museum thinking about her fortitude, the way she absorbed life even when it fell down around her, the way she welcomed a forty-year bout of solitude after losing her husband, and the way she saw color, even in total darkness, a cruel joke, dished out by a twisted hand of fate, taking her eyesight during her last fourteen years on earth.

With my own eyes, still glistening, I walked through the streets of Santa Fe, making my way past an arcade, past a five and dime store advertising Frito pie, and past Yippie Yi Yo's jewelry and souvenir shop, before crossing the street and back-stepping into a corner restaurant called Thunderbirds off Lincoln Avenue. I walked upstairs, looked the receptionist in the eye, and told her I wanted to eat outside on the balcony.

"Just one?" She asked.

"Yes," I answered thinking about Georgia O'Keeffe. She had spent the last forty years alone. I could too if needed. I glanced at the menu while soaking in the sunshine and September mountain air. I ordered the mole enchiladas. Chicken. I sat there, eating slowly, letting the explosion of O'Keeffe's color soothe me. I felt at peace,

accepting things that had happened in the past, accepting things that

I couldn't control, and coming to the realization that some things

were in my control. *Do what I can.* My mind whispered. It was time

to do something I should have done long ago – see my biological

father's property in Roswell.

#

After loading four-hundred pounds of explosives into a used 1993

Chevrolet Van, Asad removed the lock from his unit at Vinny's Self-

Storage off Mechanic Street in downtown Detroit, leaving it empty.

The van had just over two-hundred thousand miles on it, but would

serve its purpose, one that was arranged after a quick phone call to a

buddy who owned the used car lot in Detroit; although, he'd prefer

to be driving something newer and something that hadn't been

assembled in the United States. *It will have to do.* He thought.

American piece of shit. Still, he knew it would get him 620 miles to

his target. If he left now, he'd be there in ten hours. *Drive.*

#

Enola made Roswell by one in the afternoon, but not until she had

pulled over at Clines' Corners for gasoline about an hour into her drive. Her phone rang just as she maneuvered the exit. She stopped

her car in a gravel parking lot, off to the side, just in time to chat

with Allie, a conversation that led to an emotional exchange of

words that only a mother and daughter could understand, one about

missing connections, one about brothers who disappear without

notice, and one about focusing on places and people that are

available.

"It's okay Mom." She assured her mother. "Focus on you."

Something she had tried to teach Allie, but often failed to remember

herself. "I think it's great that you're going to Roswell to see

Grover's property." Enola processed his name – *Grover* – wishing

Allie and Mitch had known him and had been given the opportunity

to call him Grandpa.

"Yes, it's time." She reaffirmed Allie's supportive nature. "I

love you Allie."

"I love you too Mom." She said before talking about Shiloh

and Zeus, before sharing the day's plans, and before describing the

early morning Oregon sky – a potpourri of ash grays, burnt orange,

and smoke-tinted blues. Enola smiled, realizing Allie noticed the

sky, just as much as she did. At times, and more often than not, it seemed as if they were cut from the same mold, their senses heightened in life, each in full appreciation for every sight, smell, touch, taste, and sound. The latter echoed in Enola's mind, as she exited the gas station's parking lot, accompanied by the crunching gravel under her still new tires.

Her breathing felt relaxed as she entered Roswell, New Mexico a few hours later and traveled down Main Street to El Caporal Mexican Kitchen, where she went inside and ordered an unsweetened ice tea, and a chicken enchilada. It would be her last Mexican food for a while. She had reached her limit on Mexican food and dusty towns, but she wanted to spend a few days in Roswell, first to see her father's property, and second, to see the town she had seen in her dreams. She sat at a corner booth, eating her chicken enchilada: a large soft corn tortilla, rolled around boneless chicken that was dipped in a sweet tomato sauce, that had been made from scratch, and filled with diced onions and jalapenos. Her mouth watered for each bite, the sting of chili powder, and the soothing taste of minced cilantro tucked inside, each with a playful coating of chili pepper sauce and sour cream, as it entered the pathway lined-up directly under the roof of her mouth. She savored every bite. Slowly. Her eyes searched the table, where a stack of slips advertising a local dragonfly festival caught her attention. *Good one.* She thought, referring to the powers of the universe, and thinking back about her Roswell dream, before leaving Florida – a mass of colors lighting the way to Roswell and the feeling of being surrounded by fluttering dragonflies, their bodies various colors, and the premonition that the insects wanted her to come to New Mexico. She smiled, an attempt to control the uncanniness of the entire situation. She focused, gathering information in her head, reviewing what she knew about dragonflies. She knew the insects had long abdomens, even recalled that their bodies were divided into ten segments. *Does each segment represent a section of my life?* She questioned. Then, answering her question, she imagined she was directly between segments five and six on a life scale. Each day that passed, she knew she was moving closer to the end of her time. *Moments count.* She reminded herself and then headed for the door. She was anxious to find Grover Starks' property, her property, and had everything with her: directions from the Chaves County Property Appraisal's Office, a map, an old wooden cigar box filled with five slips of paper that she had carefully written on before leaving Florida, and a pink hand-held plastic shovel. She made her way carefully: first North Main, then One Horse Road, then Cottonwood, and finally San Juan Road. She pulled up to an area near the Bitter Lake National Wildlife Refuge, a piece of land that separated it from the rest of Roswell, where she parked her car and got out, noticing a small prairie dog make cover. No trails were welcoming her, only bits of earth begging for rain. She worked her way along the edge of the fence line separating the land from the refuge, carefully watching the placement of each step, watching for movement in the desert shrubbery that might threaten her very existence. Enola stopped at a point where dragonflies of all colors and sizes seemed to surround her. Reddish-orange spots flew through the air in front of her, attached to wings that were nearly invisible. She could tell they were dragonflies, but they looked like pieces of the sky were on fire. She knew from counting her steps and following the fence line, that she was standing on the property that Grover Starks, her father, had stood on as a boy. She removed the small backpack from her shoulders, unzipping it to pull out the thin bed-sheet, and carefully spread it on the ground. When she sat down, she realized the desert brush encased her, so she didn't move until she surveyed her surroundings and double-checked the dry soil for scorpions and rattlesnakes. None. Enola proceeded to pull out the old wooden cigar box that she had picked up at a garage sale several months prior, the same one that held her secret worries and regrets. The mid-September sun warmed her, as she dug a small hole just in front of the thin sheet that served as a barrier between her and the desert soil. She watched one of the bright orange dragonflies perched beside her on a brittle bush. She dug, all the while, feeling as if he were protecting her. Even after each slight movement that seemed to frighten him, he would return, forgiving her for any movements she had made. Enola finished digging into the rock-hard soil, then carefully opened the wooden box, before slowly pulling out the first slip of paper that had scrambled for position. She read it silently as a dark brown dragonfly sped around her.

Slip one: *I feel guilty for my mother's suicide.* She placed the tiny slip of paper into the earth, acknowledging that it was her decision, and letting the dry New Mexico soil cover her biggest regret. Gone. Slip two: *I wish I had grown up with two normal parents.* She let the second slip fall from her hand and watched it settle near the first. She thought of Dacey, his perverse urges, his hatred, his anger, his rage. She thought of Melantha's emptiness, her inability to love, and her thirst for causing pain. She wiped her tears, before reaching for the third slip of paper. Slip three: *I'm sorry I didn't get to know you Dad.* She pictured Grover Starks sitting across from her at The Veranda in Fort Myers, Florida, the first time she had ever met him face to face, the warmth in his smile, his trusting blue eyes, his strength, his character, something that leaked over to his lifelong friend, Dwayne Summons. *Strong.* She could hear Grover and Dwayne, the world's best P.I., and her dad's best friend, encouraging her as she watched a bright orange dragonfly, floating from one piece of brittle twig to another. Slip four: *I'm sorry for my own personal failures.* She looked at the tiny words written around the edge of the fourth slip, small, separated by commas, segregated by parentheses – *(my lost sister, my failed marriages, the damage to my children).* She evaluated the tiny words, phrases that represented her past. She thought about her half-sister that had ignored her phone calls and letters over the last thirty-five years. BITE. She remembered the broken men in her life. CRASH. And, she tearfully thought about her children who had to suffer the consequences of lost relationships. CUT. *I did the best I could.* The tears were blurring her vision, almost making the passing wings of a black and white dragonfly unnoticeable. Slip five: *Will I always be alone?* She wondered as she looked over at a bright orange dragonfly, hovering near, watching her, a pink plastic shovel in her right hand, her left wiping the hot tears from her eyes to clear her sight, as she gently covered her regrets and worries in the soil that once knew her father.

Enola sat there watching the dragonflies swarm around her – bits of dark brown, light blue, bright yellow, white, red, and fire-orange filled the sky. A blue-eyed dragonfly perched near her, looking at her. She thought about Melantha, her dead mother, her eyes once alive, a cold blue like the dragonfly that seemed to stare through her. Its eyes were like large blue marbles, and it had green stripes on its body and green dots on its stomach. For a moment, she could hear Melantha's voice. *You're unlovable.* She wiped more tears from her eyes with her free hand, then stood up, stronger, and the pain that had been inside of her felt like it had been set free. She imagined herself to be like the lighter colored orange dragonfly that had caught her attention. It was perched at the tip-top of a tall bush directly in front of her, its wings spread open and meticulously lined with dark orange along the edges. Then she remembered something else she knew about dragonflies. *They don't fly until they've lived more than half their lives.* Suddenly, she realized it was Grover Starks, her father who had summonsed her to the spot where she now sat. *Was it finally time to fly now?* She stood up, reaching for the dusty blue sheet, carefully folding it, bringing it back to order, picking up the empty cigar box, and soil spotted pink plastic shovel. *Thank-you Dad.* She thought. *Thanks for loving me, even when you didn't know me.* She turned away from the spot she had covered up, hiding a part of herself with her father. *Thanks for giving me hope.*

She spent the evening at Bitter Lake National Wildlife Refuge, enjoying the Dragonfly Festival she had seen advertised. She watched the faces of small children as they listened to the park ranger talk about dragonflies. One young face was covered with bits of free cotton candy, and others were smiling at the colors that swirled in the sky around the lake, where the park ranger took everybody on a five-minute walking tour. She smiled, knowing her father was out there.

Chapter Fifteen

The seventeenth of September wasn't a time for costumes.

Halloween was still over a month away, and regardless, it was not a

time for a *clown* costume, considering that there had now been six

creepy clown reports since the death of the young boy in Colorado.

Still, Azzam Al-Amin, was determined to make it to Parkwood Place

Apartments off Prospect, a Newark, New Jersey neighborhood,

where he had watched kids play down the street at Harmony

Playground, sometimes sitting for hours on a park bench, his eyes simply watching. Now, a mile away from where he knew kids would be waiting, he picked up pace, his oversized clown-shoes flopping with each step, as his bright skittle-colored hair, a mixture of blue, yellow, green, and orange, bounced along. He had seen the headlights brighten as they approached him, seen the backseat passengers, two men in their twenties, walk toward him. Although, blinded by the high-beams, he didn't see the baseball bat, until it was too late. The first swing, hit him hard, near his left temple, his only thoughts were of the children that would be disappointed he didn't show. The second swing, hit him directly on top of his skull, sending him to his knees. His last thought was for his ailing mother. He hoped the news wouldn't kill her.

Fourteen miles away, Asad was sitting in his used Chevy Van, waiting. He wanted to make sure detonation occurred at the right time, waiting for the influx of trains, his van parked in the Penn Station Garage, directly underneath the train station, 400 pounds of explosives sleeping in the back. This time there would be death. He knew the blast would be powerful; he also knew an escape plan wasn't necessary. Asad Harb would die in his father's honor. Proud. He would make Americans fearful and encourage others to follow his example. He imagined an inferno, people screaming, exploding train windows, and twisted metal. His fingers played with the metal pin attached to the bulbous shape he was holding, from his father's collection, a family heirloom. Focusing on the moment, he didn't allow himself to look at the grenade, but listened for the sound of the metal pin hitting the van door, his left hand discarding it rapidly. He shouted his final words before tossing the grenade into the sleeping explosives behind him.

"Allahu Akbar!" *God is great.*

#

When Enola May was nine years old, she went with Dacey Fears, the man she thought was her father, to a cave in the mountains west of Asheville, North Carolina. It was a cave that few people knew about, and even less attempted to enter. The walls inside the cave were lined with jagged rock, and after ten minutes in, total darkness surrounded its explorers, where bats hung from the ceiling and made their homes in the crevices. Enola could still feel the cold damp confinement, even forty-six years later. There were only two openings: an entrance, and miles from that, an exit. The walk from entrance to exit on the outside, took as long as the walk through the cave, full of treacherous landscape. The only differences were: you could see the placement of each foot and bats were not diving at your head.

Enola didn't want to go. She found the dark scary and the bats even scarier, but it was a chance to impress him. *Maybe then he won't beat me.* She rationalized in her head. So, on a Saturday morning, she followed him, first to his truck, then to the cave hidden up in the mountains, and finally inside. She wanted to hold his hand, but he was two or three paces ahead at all times. Stumbling over rocks, that she felt occasionally stab her ankles and thighs, nine-year-old Enola struggled to keep up. She followed the white t-shirt until it disappeared, but the darkness swallowed his back in front of her. It was about forty minutes into the total blackness, an hour since the beginning, when bats dove at them from all directions. High pitched screams could be heard in the pitch black, some were Enola's. Dacey yelled at her to shut up. That's when her tears fell, coating her face, like the blood that was running from her thigh, down her leg, filling her once white socks. She found it hard to breathe. The darkness stabbed at her, as bats brushed her shoulders and hair. *Shut the fuck up you baby.* She remembered him screaming causing more bats to swarm. *Turn the fuck around and wait for me until I get back to the entrance.* There was no fast way out. Dacey fought his way ahead for at least another hour while Enola stumbled in the dark back to the entrance. Alone. Bats followed her for at least twenty minutes. Their wings flapped near the side of her face. She made it back to the opening, back to the last part of daylight that was already beginning to settle into dusk. She stood there, afraid and bloody. She looked down. Both shoes were spotted with blood. Her right shoulder had a three-inch gash that she didn't even remember getting. Her thigh was sticky with blood, and her face was spotted with dirt and tears. She sat down on the ground, pulling her knees up to her chin, and waited until complete darkness surrounded her, once again. She heard him making his way through the brush that ran alongside the cave. The white t-shirt started to appear, a faint ray of moonlight notified her he was there, just before a hand grabbed a hunk of her hair. *Get the fuck up.* She remembered him saying. *Let's go.* He didn't speak to her the entire way home. Silence.

The memory was with Enola as she entered Carlsbad Cavern in New Mexico. Silence. BREATHE. There were no people ahead of her and no people behind her. *Are you sure you want to do this alone?* She remembered the park ranger ask when she showed her ticket before starting into the cavern. She had smiled and nodded yes then, but now she wasn't so sure, until she thought of Dacey Fears. She ruminated about how he made her feel – small, insignificant, helpless, and incompetent. Today, she would show him how wrong he was about her. She didn't know where he was now, or if he was even alive, but she knew he'd be seventy-seven years old if he were – an old man. She tried to vision him, his slumped posture, his tough-guy attitude, but she had no idea what he'd look like now; instead, she focused on proving to herself that she had strength inside, that he had never been able to beat out of her.

She walked carefully down the narrow path. *Stay on the path.* She remembered the park ranger tell her. *And hold onto the railing as needed or you'll fall. There's water dripping constantly into the cave.* She watched her feet disappear into the darkness. That's when she felt for the railing. The cold metal railing had absorbed the temperature inside the cave. It was in the mid-fifties by time Enola was about a half-mile in. She knew the trail wiggled to a depth of 750 feet, knew the temperature was going to keep dropping, knew to bring an extra shirt in her backpack, and knew the hike was almost two miles, so she had slipped a bottle of water in her backpack and was pacing herself. She snapped a photo of limestone shaped like cones and straws, some towering to the top of the cave, but grew leery of snapping too many photos, when she found herself surrounded by complete darkness, recognizing the movement of bats above her. She came to an area where a dimmed spotlight highlighted some of the structures formed millions of years ago, before snapping another photo with her phone. That's when she noticed about thirty bats towering above her head. She grabbed the metal railing for a moment, feeling faint, then remembered she was better than him – better than Dacey Fears. She looked up at the bats – Mexican bats like the ones she had noticed in the brochure, but kept going, deeper, further, twisting, turning, and then stopping to pull her extra shirt over her head. The warmth felt good on her arms. She didn't stop again until she reached the deepest part of the cavern. She smiled, noticing she had the option of taking an evaluator back to the surface. She did. Mission accomplished. *You didn't break me Dacey.* She thought, then made her way back to the car, and set her GPS for El Paso, Texas. *I'm still standing.*

By late evening, Enola sat down for a meal at Popeye's Chicken, pushing chunks of white juicy chicken into her mouth, and drinking down gulps of unsweet tea, reviewing her experience in the cave, and wishing she could brag to someone, just as her phone rang. It was Allie.

"Hey Mom." She said to the phone. "Did you make it to the caverns?" She asked which surprised Enola. She had forgotten how much Allie listened to her plans. She was the perfect daughter in so many ways: loving, kind, supportive, and always making her mom feel listened to.

"Yes, I did!" Enola sounded like a proud graduate.

"I knew you would Mom." Allie knew about the childhood cave story, and she also knew that she had a mother that would overcome any obstacle put in front of her. She knew that better than Enola knew it about herself. "I love you so much." And then, "I'm proud of you."

Allie was full of determination and fight, something she got from Enola, even though Enola never took the credit, and she was determined to make a life on the West Coast, where adventure and the smell of the Pacific Ocean suited her. The mother-daughter chat continued for another fifteen minutes, before Gvgeyuis were

exchanged, and ten minutes after that, Enola settled in the corner of a

parking lot in El Paso, where she shut her eyes and welcomed the

darkness. She wasn't afraid.

#

The blast at Penn Station sent a deafening sound throughout the

parking garage, and echoed for a 5-block radius. Sirens and screams

filled the air, almost simultaneously, and within minutes rescue

efforts were being conducted by local agencies, with state and

federal on its way. Search and rescue forces stepped over shattered

glass, and around deformed metal, while several units of firefighters

worked to extinguish the massive flames, still burning in the parking

garage, and in the station directly above. They worked until the

evening hours of the following day – shuffling, digging,

maneuvering, searching, and at times, shedding tears.

It wasn't until twenty-four hours had passed, that the final

tallies reached the media: forty-eight dead, including fifteen

children, one suicide-bomber killed by his own doing, 170 people

injured, some critical, an entire parking garage destroyed, several areas of the train station flattened, two trains damaged beyond repair, and forty-three cars demolished.

Asad Harb was with his father. Bobby Harb was in another dimension.

Chapter Sixteen

I stumbled along the Texas border until I found an international

entry to Mexico. It would be October in a few days, and already I

had been traveling aimlessly around the United States for nearly four

months, so I might as well wander into Mexico for the day, since I

was hugging the coast, and since my storage unit was paid for

through the end of October. I had time, so I grabbed my passport and

ID, and waited behind a row of cars. I had thought about parking on

United States soil and walking over the bridge, but two different people had discouraged me from crossing over directly into Las

Palomas: first, a lady who managed a gas station near the border,

spoke to me in broken English, *mucho murders, no safe solo* – and,

second, a United States Border Patrol officer, his words still fresh in

my head, *the cartel is all over Las Palomas*. So, I decided to cross

into Mexico at a different location, further east, and enter Ciudad

Juárez, keeping my car with me for safety. I slowly approached the

string of uniformed officers guarding the entry. They waved me

through – no passport, no ID. *Too easy.* I thought. Then, I noticed

the statue of a giant red *X* right away. I wondered its meaning, as I

drove cautiously past rows and rows of houses, all small, all needing

paint, and all with tall wrought iron fences and gates that separated

them from the dirt street, filled with potholes, stray dogs, and wild

chickens. I noticed a few stares as I traveled down the bumpy dirt

roads. Questioning stares. I tried to memorize my route, driving in

one direction – deeper into Ciudad Juárez. I stopped when I saw a

small neighborhood restaurant – white with bright red trim. It looked

like another house in the neighborhood – unassuming, and blended

in. I parked my car where I could watch it from inside. I noticed a

faded MasterCard and Visa sticker on the glass door. I pulled it open and walked in. Everybody's brown skin and brown eyes were on my white skin and blue eyes. *Dividing lines.* I thought, as I sat at a corner table and pulled a menu close then opened it. *Spanish.* Not one word of English glared at me. At least not then. Not before, a woman with dark black hair came over to me and asked me a full question in Spanish. I smiled. She caught on quickly that I only knew a few words. I stared down at the menu, spotting a familiar word I had overlooked, and happily pointed to it. Pepsi. She nodded and gave me a slight smile back. When she returned, I said thank you in Spanish the best I could.

"Gracias," I said. One of the words I knew.

"De nada." She replied as I pointed to a few other familiar words that I had spotted on the menu. Tortillas. Sopa. Pollo.

Ten minutes later I ended up with a wicker basket of steaming hot corn tortillas, a bowl of golden broth with brown rice, and a quarter piece of chicken consisting of a thigh and leg that had been seasoned in a spice I recognized, but couldn't name. Everything was delicious. I made sure the cook, who had been watching me eat, his body ducking around the kitchen wall, and the waitress, whose dark eyes and jet-black hair stood ready to collect my payment, knew I was satisfied, by smiling and patting my stomach. I signed

my charge slip. Seventy-pesos. Three-dollars and fifty-cents. A

small amount, at least half of what I would pay anywhere in the

United States. Then I remembered, *tip,* before pulling a five-dollar

bill from my purse, a concoction of cotton and linen, a picture of

Abraham Lincoln in its center, a symbol of prosperity, a necessary

evil that had provoked men to kill one another. *Money.* I thought

about the word, questioning its role in my daily life, as I looked at

the faces around me, and as I handed the piece of America to the

woman. Her smile widened, and the dividing line disappeared, if

only for a moment, as I stood in the small restaurant, a whitewashed

mixture of brick and adobe. *Does money help bring people together

or does it tear them apart?* I smiled at the simple lives that

surrounded me. *Why are some people happy with less?* I wondered.

And, *am I one of those people?*

     I spent the next five hours exploring Ciudad Juárez, while I

contemplated whether dividing lines and money were somehow

related. I ducked in the Juárez Mall, walked past a statue of Teófilo

Borunda, shopped for some small wicker baskets, and finally found a

man who spoke a little English and could explain the meaning of the giant red *X* statue, that I had seen when I crossed over the bridge, the same one that I knew marked my exit back to the USA.

"Las razas son una," he said. "Combinar." He waited to see if I understood.

"One race," I said. "Together." I could tell he agreed by the way he smiled.

"Sí, la equis," he said. For a moment I felt lost, but I recovered when he struggled for the English translation. "Yes, the *X*."

"Gracias," I said and shook his hand before getting back in my car for the final time and heading toward the giant red *X* which marked my passage home. I smiled at the impoverished country I left behind. It wasn't until I got back on U.S. soil, drove east on Interstate 10, and left Mexico in my rearview, that I thought more about the giant red *X*. *One race*. I remembered. *Human*. I knew from my childhood, from my career as a teacher, and from experiencing different people and places in the world, that good people come in all skin colors. Good people speak all languages. Good people believe in different Gods. Good people believe in different types of worship. And, good people believe in no God at all. *In God we trust.*

My thoughts traveled back to the five-dollar bill I had handed the waitress. I knew from college history, that President Dwight Eisenhower had been the one to declare that American currency would carry the motto, replacing *E pluribus unum*, Latin, meaning *out of many, one,* a short phrase and translation that I still remembered from college, and one that I've always thought promoted togetherness, like the *X* in Ciudad Juárez. Maybe the impoverished country is rich in other ways, ways that America seems to have replaced or forgotten.

Dacey Fears, and countless men and women like him, had made the world seem divided. It wasn't. It was people like Dacey who made dividing lines, and it was people like Dacey, and the father I witnessed instructing his two young children in the Oklahoma City National Memorial and Museum, which made those lines stronger. Muslims, blacks, Caucasians, Mexicans, atheists, baptists, republicans, and democrats, are all human, and each has good and evil. Each has purple dandelions.

#

Azzam Al-Amin's mother was doubled over with pain, her seventy-year-old face, a weathered mixture of broken blood vessels, wrinkles, and crow's feet, grieved into the corner of her arm, which was bent at the elbow, its sole purpose, to keep her face steady as she leaned on her son's stone coffin. The direction of her glassy, brownish-gray eyes, were fixated at an angle, one that would have met her dead son's face, had the tomb been opened for her final goodbye, but Azzam's injuries were too extreme, preventing the mortician from properly constructing Azzam's face, for the elderly Greek woman's viewing. There would be no *Kiss of Peace* placed on her son's face, before, during, or after the Trisagion Service, just the repeated phrase: *Holy God, Holy Mighty, Holy Immortal, have mercy on us.*

Kids from the Newark community, and their parents, listened as the phrase was repeated three times, and several openly wept, as they walked past the sarcophagus, placing a single white rose on its belly. The community understood that Azzam was a victim of hysteria, an example of what happens when people judge by labels – his, that of a clown. Azzam was friends with everybody in the Parkwood Place Apartments off Prospect, having lived in New Jersey most of his life, and having been the center of attention at endless kids' birthday parties. His mother was overcome with grief, when two uniformed police officers knocked on her apartment door.

Ma'am, we're sorry to inform you but Azzam was killed tonight. She

remembered both officers had to help her to a chair. *Beaten.* She

tried to focus, but was only able to hear certain words. *Baseball bat.*

Tears streamed down the elderly woman's face, then and now. An

immigrant from Lebanon. Her son, only five years old, when they

came to the United States, fleeing danger, fleeing terror that had

been a daily dosage in her young son's life, his face empty, until he

saw a clown one day at a New Jersey shopping center, then his smile

returned, and he knew from that point forward, that he would

entertain children, and be the giver of smiles. Today those smiles

were absent. Tomorrow Azzam would be lowered into the earth.

#

There were still 130 pounds of Asad's explosives unaccounted for.

Unfortunately, thirty pounds of them were on the way to a target in

Corpus Christi, Texas, right where Enola was heading.

Corpus Christi welcomed her with sidewalks that lined a

beautiful gulf coast, children played in fountain-fed water along its

path, birds fought to share trees, ships stretched out the length of a

football field in the Gulf of Mexico, and a very enjoyable seventy-two-degree October temperature filled the salt air. She parked her car and walked the sidewalk until reaching a small information center that sold mango-flavored Gatorade. She welcomed the unique taste before walking away from the concession window and before, first, chatting with the woman who appeared to be around her age behind the counter.

"Where are you from?" The woman asked, and Enola quickly recognized the fact that she still looked like she was from somewhere else. Undecided.

"Florida," Enola answered. "Near Tampa." She knew the woman probably didn't know Pasco County or New Port Richey.

"I lived in Tampa for fifteen years." The woman followed up.

"Really?" Enola couldn't read people as well as they could read her. Sometimes. "Are you familiar with New Port Richey?" Enola asked.

"Yes. I've been there many times." She answered.

"How does Corpus Christi compare to Tampa area?" Enola asked, curious about the comparison.

"Both beautiful. Both hot in the summer." The woman answered and then added, "But I think the coast of Texas gets hotter than Florida."

"Wow." Enola sounded exhausted at the thought of a summer being hotter in Texas than in Florida – more humidity. And, it was that moment, standing at the beautiful Gulf Coast of Corpus Christi that Enola made a decision and announced it to a total stranger. "I'm going back to Florida to get my stuff out of storage in Tallahassee, and then I'm moving to Spokane, Washington." She announced. The words felt good inside and out. She thought about Spokane's climate – the humidity was much lower than what she was accustomed to, the mountains guarded over it but didn't invade the city's personal space, rainfall was actually less in Spokane than it was in Florida, and the cold air made Enola feel alive. She wanted to try it. She craved it.

"Oh, it's so beautiful out there." The woman added. "I'd live there if my family wasn't here." Enola heard the passion in the woman's voice, especially when she mentioned the word *family*. Enola thought about her last conversation with Allie – the one where Allie talked about loving Oregon. Then she thought about her last *real* conversation with Mitch – before he boarded an Atlantic Ocean bound cargo ship – one where he shared that he'd like to live in Nevada someday. She pictured herself living in Washington State, close enough to make it to the coast of Oregon in nine hours, and close enough to make it to the Nevada state line in ten. The decision of living where she was within reasonable distance to both adult children excited her. Finally, she knew where she was headed. She inhaled the Gulf of Mexico into her lungs, holding the smell of seaweed and salty fish inside, until she felt the indecisiveness that had been consuming her disappear. It was a moment of celebration, one marred by forty-foot, vividly colored orange flames, that lit up the Corpus Christi skyline.

Chapter Seventeen

Rodney Lakin climbed up the small metal ladder behind the tanker

truck's cab. The driver, was inside the gas station, grabbing a short

restroom break and a cup of coffee – black. He didn't see the man

who had been following him, tailing his fuel tanker. Lakin, fifty-

nine, used to transport diesel fuel, and he was familiar with how to

jimmy open a valve. Within seconds, he had the valve open, his

hands steady, as he rarely trembled, the only sign of being unsteady

was in his mind, as he worried that the driver might return before he was finished. He attached an exploding Bridge-wire detonator

(EBW), and quickly climbed down from the top of the tanker,

making his way back to his vehicle. He didn't care about the lives he

would be destroying. He was angry. Pissed off that a company he

had worked with for twenty-three years would fire him because of

getting his first DUI. Drinking and driving wasn't something Rodney

Lakin ever did. He explained it before the personnel board. *I drove*

my pregnant wife to the hospital. He remembered explaining. *I had*

consumed three, maybe four beers. The board members faces were

judgmental. He recalled their questions: *You couldn't get a friend or*

neighbor to drive? One asked. *You were risking her life and your*

unborn child's life. Another stated. *Why didn't you call an*

ambulance? It didn't matter that he explained. *We lived too far away*

from neighbors. Time was of an essence. She was in pain. I couldn't

find my cell phone. And then, *we lost the baby.* It was then, after

leaving his wife at the hospital, after she was finally sedated, and

after he held his stillborn baby daughter, that he left the hospital, just

to clear his head, but was pulled over by a police officer. Now,

Rodney Lakin was angry. No job. No baby. And, his wife barely

carried on a conversation anymore. This time someone would listen.

He knew the EBW would go off the moment the tanker went over a small bump, just a gentle slap. Something his baby never received.

#

I felt like a small breath of fresh air entered my soul. I welcomed a new beginning, starting over in the Pacific Northwest. I called Allie to let her know I had made a final decision on where to move. She was excited that I had settled on Spokane, Washington, a place she could travel to without much difficulty, even if they ended up going to California instead of staying in Oregon. I hungered for the large swallows of cold crisp air, yearned for trails and parks that I had never been to before, and a sea of new faces. After calling Allie, I hung up to call Dixie.

"Hey girl, what are you up to?" I asked when I heard her voice.

"About five-four." She laughed.

"I have a favor." I went straight there.

"Anything." She said.

"Are you and Ryan still leaving for about eight days to go to a race in Louisiana?"

She remembered Dixie talking about the fact that Ryan was going to race his muscle car, his pride and joy, second to her of course.

"Yes, Ryan can't wait." She said with excitement. They didn't leave North Carolina too often.

"Is it okay if I volunteer for the dog sitting duty while you're gone?" I asked hoping her tone would ease my mind.

"Kobie and Josie would love that!" I could tell she did too. She loved her labs more than Ryan loved his muscle car.

"Great," I said. Then added, "I need a place to unwind and get organized while I gear up to drive another three thousand miles." I hoped the announcement wouldn't be a shock to her.

"I told Ryan you were going to move there." She quickly replied as I wondered where she was even talking about. "I could hear it in your voice – when you called from Spokane." I laughed into the phone. She knew me better than I knew myself.

"I gave it away already?" I asked playfully.

"You sounded happy when you were there Nola." She said.

"I think I can make a go of it there Dix," I said.

"It will be a long plane trip for us to see each other, but we will." I thought about how long we had been friends as she continued talking. I remembered how nervous I was in first grade, moving from Detroit to Asheville, standing in front of the class introducing myself at six years old, and hoping no one would laugh at me. No one did, and one person smiled – Dixie.

"Thanks for letting me stay at your house Dix." I wanted her to know how much I appreciated her. "I'll look in on your mom for you too." I thought about her mom, a few miles down the street, alone, having a hard time with her breathing lately. Old age.

"Oh Nola." She said. "She'd love that."

We hung up the phone, and I could feel the biggest move of my life starting to take form. I thought of René in New Port Richey, a friend I had only known a few years, but someone I trusted, someone who had let me stay with her after my apartment lease expired in Florida. I called her next. Thinking about all my mail that had been on hold at the post office where I had a box. Maybe she would send it to me, while I'm at Dixie's.

"Hey René." She answered by the third ring.

"Hey Enola." She didn't know I liked Nola.

"I've finally made a decision about where I'd like to live," I said.

"Washington?" She announced before I told her.

"Yes." I laughed at the fact that everybody knew before me.

"I knew by your Facebook posts that you loved it the most." She explained.

"I want to give it a try there René," I said.

"That's great." She answered supportively.

"Do you think you could go by the post office off Main Street and get all my mail? Maybe send it to me while I'm taking care of Dixie's labs for a week?" I hated asking but I didn't have anyone else in New Port Richey who I thought would do it.

"Don't you have to go by your storage unit in Tallahassee to get your stuff?" She answered my questions with a question.

"Yes," I said. Then remembering that I had laid awake in the Walmart lot last night sorting out my route I replied. "I'm in Texas now. I'm going to continue to hug the coast, go by and clean out my storage unit, and then head up to North Carolina." I explained. "After that I'll figure out which route is best to travel depending on the weather." I thought about which roads might be dangerous –

disguised with snow or ice during October.

"I will go by and get all your mail, and then I'll bring it to

you in Tallahassee if you'll stay with me in a hotel for a night or

two." She said. "Maybe dinner and exploring?" She added on in the

form of a question. That's when I knew why I liked her. She had a

zest for life.

"René, you are wonderful!" I exclaimed. "I would absolutely

love that." I wanted more friends like René and Dixie.

I finished my conversation with René and followed 35 North

to Port Lavaca, Texas. It wasn't dark when I got there, only late

afternoon, but I knew stopping was something I needed to do. I

hadn't slept too much the night before. I needed to close my eyes

and let my body rest. I hoped the breeze would blow from the port

and into my car. A good night's sleep would be priceless.

#

Enola made it to Galveston, Texas the next day by noon. She drove

to the beach on the east end, parked the car on the side of a dirt road,

hiked over a mound of dirt and wildflowers, kicked off her New

Balance lime green flip-flops, and stuck her feet in the Gulf of

Mexico. She sucked in energy from the salt air, hot sun, and large metal barges and ships that lined the coast. It was a beautiful October day.

She was different inside – much more relaxed, full of peace, and the only thing she felt inside was a warm flutter. STIR. She looked out at the blue-green water thinking of Mitch and remembering how he worked on lift boats in the Gulf of Mexico for almost six years. *I hope he finds peace in his life someday, and gets to feel the same serenity I feel right now.* She thought.

Hours passed before Enola made her way further inland – to Pasadena just east of Houston. She found a twenty-four-hour Walmart and a Starbucks off Spencer Highway, ducked into the Starbucks, ordered a venti very-berry-hibiscus and sat in a corner booth to play on her laptop. She didn't want to push herself; she needed to store as much mental energy as possible so she could make major decisions about moving: whether to get a hitch on her car so she could pull a small trailer, which route to take back to the West Coast, and finding an apartment. So, tonight she would take it easy – sipping her berry-hibiscus, researching on her laptop, and sleeping as soon as darkness fell on Pasadena, Texas.

The next morning, she traveled about an hour before stopping at a Planet Fitness in Beaumont, Texas. She felt refreshed after doing a couple of miles on the treadmill and taking a hot shower. The sky darkened around her, so she ducked into the Parkdale Mall, grabbed a seafood dinner in the food court consisting of fish, two large butterfly shrimp, and three oysters. She ate all the seafood except for the oysters; she couldn't get past the first one – too slimy inside.

She wasn't in a hurry to travel far, especially with the pending list of things she had to do – let her storage unit know she would be there in a few days, research hitches for her Hyundai, and find an apartment in Spokane. Busy work? Yes. A needed change? Yes. Challenging? Yes, especially after finding out her car really shouldn't tow anything, not that distance. *No hitch.* She decided. She would have to fit everything inside her car, which meant half of her stuff wouldn't be allowed to go. Deep breath. She let the night close in around her, before closing her eyes to the end of another day.

Enola made Louisiana by noon the following day. Jennings, Louisiana was going to be her stopping point, but something made her drive on – to Lafayette. It felt welcoming – the people friendly – Cajun spice filled the afternoon air. Enola pulled into T-Coon's, a spicy, Cajun lunch hot-spot. She ordered from sight: smothered pork cooked Cajun style, rice, broccoli, and potato salad. Her appetite had grown, like her excitement to start a new life. She was bent on Washington State, set on a little apartment with a balcony or patio, longed for the mountain air, and thirsted for life, the one that was flaming inside of her.

Even though Enola felt revived, she still knew she was playing by the seat of her pants. The part that made Enola the most anxious was locating an apartment. *Where?* She wondered. Her actions put up a good fight – swinging into a coffee shop across from T-Coon's to get on the internet and look at apartments in the Spokane area. She wrote down the contact information for ten different apartments in Spokane, all near neighborhoods that she remembered liking, and then placed stars by the few complexes she recalled seeing when she had spent a couple days in Spokane. Tomorrow she would call a few more places, and the next day, and the next, until like everything else in her life, it would eventually work out.

#

Rodney Lakin read the news article from his living room chair, twice, the face of the forty-year-old tanker driver seemed to glare back at him, his photo above the article, a family man, leaving behind a wife and two toddlers. Beside the tanker driver's image, was another snapshot, that of a young single mother with her five-year-old daughter sitting on her lap, the driver and passenger of the car adjacent to the tanker, as it moved slowly over the railroad tracks, a crossing point at North Port Avenue, and its final resting spot. BOOM. It was not the result he wanted. He hadn't meant to hurt innocent people; his intentional plan killed unintentional targets. His hands trembled uncontrollably, as he read the article a third time. *Hazmat team responded.* He thought about the damage. The lives lost. *A father. A single mother. A little girl.* His hand, still trembling, pulled the small end-table drawer open, a hidden, and somewhat decorative drawer, that held his loaded 22-caliber Cobra Derringer.

He placed the barrel to his right temple, and pulled the trigger.

Chapter Eighteen

I rolled into New Orleans two days later, found my way to Fulton

Parking Garage and parked on the fourth floor. Number 445. I made

my way to the elevator and walked Fulton until I hit Canal Street. I

looked at the shops and restaurants along the way, stopping

occasionally to take a picture.

Bourbon Street met Canal at a CVS Pharmacy that reached to

the sky. People hustled like ants down the sidewalk, most avoiding

eye contact. I adjusted my walk down Bourbon, carefully stepping over broken pieces of sidewalk, and trying not to concentrate on the strong smell of urine. A man wearing a full-length chiffon gown, Victorian-style, looked like he just stepped out of the Deadwood Saloon, as he leaned against the outside of a small bar. A slit showed his nyloned thighs – toned and muscular. He smiled at me, careful not to tilt his head, in order to keep his hat, that fronted a sheer black veil, upright. I could see his jawline, smooth, hairless, and carefully powdered in ivory. His eyes were green and popped with the well-applied black mascara. He looked like a china doll. I noticed his neck was wide with a protruding Adam's apple. He held his stance as I walked by. Signs about two-for-one and flavored daiquiris surrounded me. I thought about stopping for a bite to eat, but I didn't want to contend with the smell of piss, beer, and liquor. I kept walking, thinking about the last two days of researching apartments and making phone calls. Numerous inquiries about one-bedroom apartments in Spokane. The apartments that I had suspected might work, were either too expensive, or not available anytime soon. I tried not to become frustrated, remembering that eventually everything would play out. *Stay focused.* I reminded myself. I did. I kept walking, the air sticky for October, and my hair that once smelled like coconut, now smelling like Bourbon Street.

I should have stopped for a shower, as the fall heat wave and sweat coated my skin, but I didn't. I drove until I was about thirty minutes outside of New Orleans, before stopping at a Planet Fitness lot in Slidell. Not wanting to be part of the night patrons, I crawled into the back of my car, anticipating an early morning go at the treadmill and shower, but two hours into a sweaty night's sleep, I felt the presence of a car behind me. My discreet glance revealed a white four-door SUV marked Slidell Police. I panicked. I guess I didn't have a reason to panic, but I didn't want to admit I was sleeping in my car, that I had nowhere to go, and that I was in transition. So, I hid under my blankets, turned my fan off, and let the humid October take over, until I heard the sound of a vehicle pulling away. Fifteen minutes had passed before it simply left. By that point, I was too spooked to attempt sleep again and too hot. I used Google Maps to find my way back to 10 East and drove with my windows down, allowing the night air to dry my sticky pores. It wasn't long before I saw the Mississippi state line and a welcoming center that offered twenty-four-hour restrooms and security. I felt happiness inside my weary body, as I pulled in, grabbed a washcloth and my container of

pump Dial soap and went inside. I gave myself a birdbath within

minutes (a description I had heard truckers use when they didn't

have time for a full shower), using a stall for privacy to take off my

clothes and hit every area of my body with my washcloth. I pulled

on a fresh bra and t-shirt, clean underwear and my favorite pair of

jeans, the ones that were old and faded and had a hole exposing my

left knee. I felt some relief as I welcomed the darkness in the back of

my car and shut my eyes. There was no reason to wake up until

daylight. I knew there were other drivers resting near me in their

cars, a place where grabbing sleep wouldn't be challenged, but I

couldn't sleep, my mind craved the sound of rippling waves, the

hypnotizing in-and-out waterline, made by the Gulf of Mexico's

signature. I jumped back on I-10, until I saw a sign directing me to

turn right, offering an access road to the beach. I knew salt air was a

cure-all for me. I took the exit, traveled about fifteen minutes, until I

could smell it. No announcement was needed. I caught a glimpse of

the Pass Christian, Mississippi shoreline in front of me as the three-

a.m. moon bounced off the water. I pulled my car into a parallel

parking spot and grabbed my phone, as I exited the car.

Sand brushed over my flip-flops in the moonlight as I walked toward the rushing sound of water. I felt alive. I breathed in the air. It wasn't humid like I had been suffering in. It offered a sense of freedom. I walked for about fifteen minutes down the beach, unable to see further than the distance of my hand in the moonlight. Waves hit the sand in a soothing rhythm. I lowered myself to the sandy surface, feeling the scattered graveyard of broken shells with my hands, searching the darkness for lost treasure. Something cold and hard caught the attention of the fingertips on my right hand. Pulling it to my face, I could see the wavy dark brown lines, some bold, others broken in mid-stream, but its shape identifiable, even in the fading moonlight. *Mossy-Ark.* I recalled, having spent years studying different seashells and their names. *A lot like the Turkey Wing, only bigger.* I reminded myself. I grasped it in my hand, carrying it back to my car, and with a new burst of energy, I made my way to 90 East. Some nights weren't made for sleep.

I didn't stop again until reaching Long Beach, where nightfall finally allowed the sun to share a small piece of sky, and seagulls that had been huddled together throughout the night took flight in the pre-dawn hours. I watched the clouds gently shower the new day, my driver's window down, allowing the prickly rain to poke at my left arm and hand. I felt alive, even though my night's sleep had been unsuccessful.

Accepting the fact that the time for sleep had passed, I drove, making Biloxi. By that point, I decided I had driven enough, even though it wasn't even noon. I stopped at the Riverdale Mall, walked to the food court, where I ordered a Styrofoam container of Lo Mein Noodles and spicy chicken. I felt the need to let sleep takeover, but I fought it like a child avoiding a nap. Not until I had completed one load of laundry, two miles on a treadmill at a new gym location, a thirty-minute shower, and drank down two glasses of green iced-tea, did I finally attempt to sleep, which by that point, was nine p.m. This time, I made sure my windows were down an extra inch on all sides, a standing invitation to the slight breeze that played with the salty air, as I shut my eyes in the back of a Walmart lot off 90 East. My mind settled, and long overdue sleep took over.

#

Enola's life had been about downsizing – material items, the number of people she lived with, and now her responsibilities. She made a phone call to U-Haul from Pascagoula, Mississippi just to reverify her options. Getting a hitch on the back on her Hyundai was doable; getting to Washington State with a transmission was not. She knew she had no other option except to downsize again, unless she rented a small U-Haul truck and pulled her car, but the prices she was getting for that option, made it where it wasn't an option, at least in Enola's opinion. *I'll figure it out.* She calmed herself.

By the time she reached Mobile, Alabama it was nearly five p.m., but she had gotten a lot done. She had stopped at a St. Vincent De Paul Thrift shop along the way, leaving behind her futon mattress that had once filled the width and length of every available space behind her driver's seat, a place where she fought to keep clothes neatly stacked, and a place where pillows and blankets had been shoved in remaining corners, because of the unexpected humidity and heat, making them less desirable. After creating space and being fairly organized, she stopped at a car wash, but not to wash her car, the Mississippi rain had done that for her six hours earlier; instead, she was there to use the vacuum. Four and a half months of traveling equaled a very dirty car, and she knew being organized and clean was step one. Step two was getting to her storage unit in Florida in a few more days. She had been rehearsing one simple question with preassigned answers over and over: *Can you purchase this item again in Washington? Yes – toss it. No – keep it.*

For now, though, she would explore Mobile, Alabama. She drove through downtown, pulling over several times to admire tall buildings with different architectural shaped panes of glass, metal that hugged corners and curves, and block that molded each building into a unique piece of artwork. For Enola, the shape of buildings and layout of a city, made her feel scattered or comfortable. She hoped her memories of Spokane were spot-on. *I felt comfortable there.* She reminded herself, as she went back to concentrating on driving. Florida would welcome her tomorrow.

#

Creepy clown reports were diminishing, even though Halloween was only two weeks away. Enola noticed that now, the local newspapers and radio-news reports were focused on the aftermath of recent Hurricane Matthew and the damage it had done to Jacksonville Beach. The slap from the Cat-2 left downed trees and several flooded areas. Enola sighed. *I'm not going to miss the threat of hurricanes.* She thought as she took the exit to Tallahassee. It was just after twelve noon. She pulled through a drive-up down the street from her storage unit, ordering one of her usual's – a very berry hibiscus – then called René, to see if she had started her four-hour drive. She had. One hour ago. *Three more hours.* Enough time for Enola to reduce a five-by-five storage unit to the available space in her Hyundai Elantra. She pulled onto the property of Extra Space Storage, working her way down the fourth row, to unit forty-seven, then exited her car, and placed the white key inside the lock that had guarded her valuables. An assortment of Rubbermaid containers, some black, some silver, and some light blue, faced her. They were surrounded by wall art – too big to fit in any of the containers – a footstool, a black table big enough to hold a large potted plant, a white plastic laundry basket, and a fishing pole that Allie and Reese had given her before they left Florida. She took a mental inventory and then decided action was the best method. Moving stuff around, she pulled out the Rubbermaid containers first – pulling off lids and setting them aside. She glanced inside at pieces of her life: a kitchen knife set from Mitch, a large pepper bottle from Allie shaped like the Eifel Tower, a gray Victoria Secret's robe that felt like a kitten's fur, a small heart-shaped glass bottle from Allie that she had filled with sand and tiny shells to remind her of their trip to Venice Beach together, a hummingbird shower curtain that she had gotten at Home

Goods almost two years ago with ceramic shower curtain hooks that

had a hummingbird painted on each, hangers, clothes, shoes, and

what seemed like endless reminders of the past. She studied the

inside of her Hyundai. *Six Rubbermaid containers, my wall art, and*

maybe some lose items to fill every nook and cranny. She thought, as

her hands remained busy, maneuvering items from one container to

another. Two hours passed before she had a pile for The Salvation

Army and three empty Rubbermaid containers. *Six containers left.*

She noticed a young couple six-or-seven units down trying to

organize their stuff into their unit, so she walked the three empty

containers to them.

"Would you like these containers?" She asked as she

approached.

"We would love them." The woman answered back. A look

of gratitude was on her face as she refolded a pile of clothes in front

of her. "Thanks so much." She extended her hand and smiled.

"No problem," Enola replied, then started to turn away.

"Let me know if you need help lifting anything." The woman's voice followed Enola as she walked back to everything she owned.

"Thanks." Enola turned to say. "I appreciate the offer."

Enola then loaded the Salvation Army pile into her car, allowing a mixture of loose items, that had claimed a spot over the last couple of hours to stay, before replacing the bins that had advanced from the elimination process, back into the storage unit, where they would patiently wait, while she made a trip to the Salvation Army, where the loose items that had prematurely hitched a ride would find themselves up for possible rejection once again. *I'll replace the footstool.* She thought. *I can buy a new table for a plant.* She reminded herself. *I don't need to keep that laundry basket.* She told herself. Old shoes. *Replaceable.* Several shirts that she didn't like. *Replaceable.* Old plastic hangers. *Replaceable.* The shower curtain and hooks. *Replaceable.* And, *I need to change my theme anyhow.* A mirror that she used to hang in the bathroom. *Replaceable.*

When Enola got back to the storage unit and slid the metal door up above her head she stood there. It was an emotional moment. A part of her wondered if there were more items inside the surviving containers that she should part with, another part of her felt embarrassed that she was fifty-five years old and owned very little, and a yet another part of her felt something new for the first time – a sense of freedom from materialism and a feeling that she had just been reborn. The items in that five-by-five unit didn't represent her. She stood there staring at the containers that were left, but her eyes didn't see them. Instead they saw her childhood street in Detroit, her elementary school in Asheville, the insurance company where her childhood hospital used to be, and a rainbow over the mountains of Durango, Colorado. She felt the icy water hitting her face from Niagara Falls, tasted the Vietnamese food she had in Oklahoma City, heard the sound of the cathedral's bells in Santa Fe, felt her son's arm around her in Little Rock, inhaled the bone-chilling rain in Glacier National Park, and smelled the aftermath of endless Bourbon Street parties. She moved her eyes slowly through the maze of containers, imagining cornfields and rolled bales of golden hay. She let the buffalo and bighorn sheep pass before her and dark caverns swallow her, and she felt the flutter of a dragonfly inside, but it was gentle, like Allie's touch, and moved slowly like the hot air balloons that bounced in the Colorado sky. It was like she had an epiphany, an awakening, and was no longer associating herself with stuff or places. She was completely free.

The new Enola picked up one container after another, fitting them like puzzle pieces into her car. She smiled, thinking of Allie and the s'mores they had roasted in Yellowstone, her containers represented the marshmallow, one side of her car symbolized chocolate, and the other side, a crispy graham cracker. For a moment, she wanted to laugh, but then she felt tears sliding down her cheeks, as she looked at the empty five-by-five room, one last time, her mind picturing the uninhabited Indian cliff dwellings in Colorado. She pulled the metal door down. Emptiness could be heard, but it wasn't felt. *Together.* She remembered. *Human race.* Glancing at the red illumination on her car's dashboard. Her last thought was of the red *X* in Ciudad Juárez, before meeting René.

Chapter Nineteen

René and Enola pulled into the Best Western in Tallahassee around the same time.

"I can't believe you drove four hours just to see me," Enola said to the woman, a few years older, an infectious smile painted across her face, and her blond hair hitting the top of her shoulders.

"I didn't want to miss seeing you Enola," René said. She reached out to give Enola a hug. Enola wasn't used to people going out of their way for her. She knew Dixie would, but she rarely asked for favors. She didn't want to put anyone out. Ever. Still, she wondered how many people would drive four hours to see her.

Dixie? Yes. *Allie?* Definitely. *Mitch?* Maybe. *Anyone else?* Probably not.

After a few hours of chatting like teenage girls inside room 104 about René's upcoming retirement, places they'd both like to travel, and the ups and downs in life, they made their way down the street to Cabo's Grill, where surfboards of assorted colors hung from the ceiling and hamburgers as big as saucers made their way to tables underneath. People laughed, waitresses smiled, and the atmosphere was warm and relaxing.

"I can't believe you're moving to Washington state," René said as she bit her hamburger and eyed her side of fries.

"It's a big move," Enola commented. "But I need a fresh start." She stabbed a bite of pasta salad which included a vegetable that she knew was *heart of palm*, but had only tried one other time in her life. "New people. Mountains. Snow. New experiences."

"You're going to have a lot of fun." René followed up. "*New* looks good on you."

They talked most of the night about how some people don't take chances, won't take chances, how change is scary, and how change pumps you full of adrenaline. Enola lusted for that adrenaline.

The next day Enola and René went to St. Mark's National Wildlife Refuge. Butterflies bounced from wildflower to wildflower, a bright red cardinal made its way to a tree in front of Enola, reminding her of Mitch and how they spotted one at the Little Rock Zoo, dragonflies swooped down from the sky looking for mosquitoes, an eight-foot alligator lay off in the swamp not far from the hiking trail, and a butterfly floated nearby like a highly trained synchronized swimmer. They walked quietly, snapping photos of everything they saw and of each other. Enola let her guard down, enjoying everything – sunshine, conversation, the middle of a new day, and the beginning of a new part of her life – moving to Spokane.

They stayed up late watching comedy shows that night in room 104. Enola laughed her way to sleep and woke up the next morning with an appetite for life, for food, and for friendship. She had breakfast with René at the Canopy Road Café, and after shifting some things around in her car for a better line of vision, she knew it was time to say goodbye and make her way to 312 North, a little road that wiggled its way through Georgia.

Enola called Dixie after realizing she only had five more hours to drive before reaching Asheville, North Carolina. Dixie sounded happy to hear from her, excited that she might arrive by nine p.m.

"I miss you," Dix said. "Get here safely. It doesn't matter how late." She reassured Enola.

"Thanks Dix." And then, "I'll call you if I see I'm running past nine." She smiled at the phone, smiled at a forty-nine-year friendship, and drove toward mountains that disappeared in the dark sky. This time she didn't feel smothered. She welcomed every curve that moved beneath her.

#

The forty-six-year-old South Carolina woman, sat hours in her small apartment, working like a surgeon, her hands performing meticulously, making sure that each package was rigged to detonate when opened. She mailed one to President Barack Obama, the second to the governor of South Carolina, and the third to her local

Social Security Office. The packages were heavy enough to peak the interests on the receiving end, but light enough to remain inconspicuous, a normal part of that day's mail delivery. Usually, the governor of South Carolina didn't open his mail, but his secretary had taken the day off, and his curiosity got the best of him. He thought about tearing the top of the package, but like all areas of his life, he believed in keeping order, so he reached for a letter opener, carefully pulling the small box from its wrapping, and last minute, deciding to seek entry from the end of the box, instead of the top. When he looked inside, he knew his point of entry saved his life. Carefully, he sat the box down, backed out of the room, and made a beeline to the closest phone, but the bomb squad was already at his door, before he could even dial.

#

I stayed at Dixie's house until the morning of Halloween. The first week was with her, Ryan, and their two labs: Josie and Kobie. Ryan worked in his office each day, while Dix and I roamed around Asheville: Ross, Culver's for a hamburger, her mom's house, and Merrimon Avenue looking at pumpkin displays. We talked about everything – how we'd laugh during sleepovers, what other elementary friends were doing with their lives, and how, through all the changes in life, we were always friends. Sisters. The blood sister I never got to know as an adult was a gift I received with Dixie.

The second week, I watched Dixie and Ryan drive away, Ryan's truck pulled an enclosed trailer, with a 1967 Camaro safely tucked inside. Dix was happy I was there to watch the house and look after Josie and Kobie; I was happy I was there to use the internet and find an apartment in Washington State. And, I needed the week to absorb silence, and a little downtime. No road in front of me that teased me to follow it. But, by the time the week passed, I was itching for open road once again.

Dix and Ryan arrived home late Saturday night. I was proud of the fact that I had held things together while they were gone, had passed a one week test to see if I still had a domestic side to me, had successfully made chicken-a-la-king one night, and a skillet meal of squash, tomatoes, and steak tenderloin another, had washed several loads of laundry, had vacuumed, swept, watered plants, taken Dix's mom out for lunch one day, and had delivered her a 1000 piece puzzle the next. I let Asheville soak into my soul, car windows down, exploring Patton Avenue and downtown Biltmore. But now, I was anxious to spend one more full day with Dixie and then hit open road, something I knew I was good at.

Sunday, we made our way to Merrimon Avenue in Asheville, stopping at a hill of bright orange pumpkins, colorfully displayed at the Episcopalian Church. Haystacks served as guards, giving the church a medieval-castle look, creating a pumpkin-patch that looked like a magical land. Ryan went with us, which was fun, and the three of us, together, laughed our way through a series of photos, some with our tongues out and eyes squinted. The sun bounced off the bright orange patch of pumpkins, like our laughter, uncontained. The laughing worked up an appetite, so we made our way to Bellagio's down the street. I had Greek pasta, Dix had meat lasagna, and Ryan had a large Greek salad with grilled chicken. I stole glances of the two of them together. Thirty-five years of marriage. Obviously, they were doing something that worked.

We stopped for ice cream on the way back to their house, sundaes – piled with chocolate fudge syrup, whipped crème, walnuts, and a bright red cherry on each. By the time we parked in their driveway, Kobie and Josie were anxiously barking for attention, and darkness had fallen overhead. We thought about calling it a night, but I knew, just like they did, that tomorrow I would be leaving early and our next visit might be years away, so we changed to swimsuits and submerged ourselves in the hot tub on the deck out back, underneath a sky of stars, a half-moon, and night air that had reached the mid-sixties.

I let the cold air become part of my face as the three of us chatted about Mitch and Allie, about Spokane, and about just enjoying life. It was almost midnight before Ryan stepped out of the hot tub, leaving Dix and I for a few more minutes of conversation.

"I want you to be careful out there," Dix said.

"I will," I assured her. "I have to give this a try." I followed up.

"I know you do." She said. "But, if you don't like it, don't forget your home is here."

"I know," I answered, even though I didn't. That was a feeling I had missed out on my entire life, but I imagined if home were people, then Asheville would always be my home, at least one of them, another would always be near Allie.

We got out, grabbed towels, and fought our way through cold air that blocked us. I slept better than I expected that night, almost seven hours, before getting up, before sliding on clothes that I had laid out the night before, and before tapping on Dixie's bedroom door to tell her goodbye. She insisted on walking me to my car, and hugged me tightly before I reached for my car door, as I hid tears that ran down my face. I didn't want her to see a weak side to me. She thought I was strong, so I didn't want her to know otherwise. I pulled away, extending my arm out the driver's window, and waving to my friend of forty-nine years. A lifetime.

I made my way to 40 West, and was in Tennessee before I realized it. I jumped off 40 West around Knoxville, taking little roads that ran along the south end of Tennessee, once dipping into Georgia, and then back into Tennessee, and finally into Chattanooga. I stopped to look at the Tennessee River and Nick-a-jack River, both lined with trees bursting in orange, red, yellow, and various shades of light and dark browns. The last day of October showed its colors. I drove with the windows down, and didn't stop except to pee or grab an ice tea, until Memphis. Then I found a Walmart, where I knew I could grab a few hours in my car, this time, without a futon, my seat slightly tilted, fighting for position with Rubbermaid containers. *I will make do.* I remembered thinking before shutting

my eyes.

#

ATF Associate Deputy Director Bosman was smiling in his Detroit

office. News of the South Carolina woman's arrest, and the recovery

of the explosives spread quickly throughout the field office. It wasn't

the amount that made him smile. It was the fact, that his meticulous

records, and the investigative work conducted by his team and FBI

agents, was finally paying off. Shortly after the Penn Station

bombing, his men were able to piece things together. First, they were

able to identify Asad Harb as the suicide bomber in Penn Station.

Second, from ransacking his home in Detroit, they discovered he

was the one who had taken the 930 pounds of explosives off the

CSX train in April. And, finally, agents were able to ascertain who

had received the explosives, information they read from Asad Harb's

ledgers, the saving grace for President Obama's office, the Social

Security office in South Carolina, and the reason the bomb squad

was at the governor's door, before he even had a chance to make a

phone call. They would have been there sooner, had it not taken so

long to interrogate the woman who had mailed the three boxes. And, now, after endless hours of investigation, pouring over Asad's

records, and matching up buyers with nearby explosions and

recoveries, Associate Deputy Director Bosman was able to estimate

how many pounds of explosives were still unaccounted for, *between*

fifty and one-hundred, he thought, and those recipients' locations,

somewhere in Kansas and somewhere in Montana. He was in the

ballpark. Eighty-five pounds of explosives, from the CSX robbery,

were still out there. But he was wrong about one thing – recipients

are mobile.

Chapter Twenty

Enola drove through Arkansas, trying to control her emotions, and

trying not to think about the fact that she hadn't heard from Mitch

since he boarded the cargo ship in New York. She wondered where

he was now, trying to picture him, operating a crane somewhere in

the Atlantic Ocean. *A year.* She remembered his estimation. *Surely,*

he won't be gone a year. She imagined him, his face unshaven, and

his body becoming a man she wouldn't recognize. Visions of

holding him as a baby played out on the highway in front of her: first a baby, then a toddler, then a young boy, age five or six, his posture in crouching position, often assumed during tee-ball, mostly hunting for crickets, and a mile further down the highway, more memories unfolded, as if she were sitting in a theater watching a giant screen – rooting for their NFL teams together, his crooked smile, his dark brown eyes, and his propensity for building and art design – the clay castle he had built her when he was in middle school, a framed display of a song he had written and dedicated to her as a late teen, and a four-foot piece of nautical rope that he had expertly tied to show several different boating knots as a young adult. She missed him and wanted to be part of his life. Visions turned to tears, as she drove away from Little Rock, Arkansas. They followed her for at least fifty miles. She pulled over about an hour before reaching Oklahoma City to get an ice tea and wash her face in a Waffle House bathroom. She pulled out her cell phone, checking her GPS, and decided going into Oklahoma City wasn't necessary. *Take a hard right*. She thought, then made her way to 165 North, then 412 West, and finally 35 North before stopping, right as night fell. She had been driving persistently, trying to get her emotions in order, before realizing the day was being swallowed, and hunger had been overlooked. She pulled into a Phillips 66 off 35 North, grabbed a

tuna sandwich from Subway, and parked in a dark area of the

parking lot. Maybe she could catch five hours of sleep without being

asked to leave. She closed her eyes just as the rain started to come

down. Hard.

#

Douglas Brandt lived in a home that was falling down around him in

Wichita, Kansas. The city had threatened to condemn it several

times, by the second day in November, they had, and by the third

day in November, the FBI and the Bureau of Alcohol, Tobacco, and

Firearms stood in the condemned home, full of debris and clutter,

but absent of any explosives. Too late. *Dammit. It's roaming the*

streets. Bosman processed the thought in his head after getting the

news. Now, they had thirty-pounds of explosives, according to Asad

Harb's records, somewhere out there with Douglas Brandt.

Somewhere.

#

I woke up just after four in the morning, not to noise, just to the cold.

Forty-seven degrees fought its way into my Hyundai, where I had

crawled under the only three blankets I owned. Cold and awake, I reached for the lever on my driver's seat, which I pulled to sit

upright, no longer able to fully enjoy the extended version of

sleeping in my car, where a once comfortable futon mattress had

been replaced with Rubbermaid containers. Now comfort wasn't

possible, but I had managed since leaving Dixie's house, without

seeking the security of a motel, and without spending any money on

lodging. I wanted to make the money I had in my checking account

last as long as possible. My first month's rent, furniture, a small

television, and more winter clothes would take everything I had left.

I went in the Pilot gas station to use the restroom and grab a

hot chocolate, before finding my way in the dark to the entrance

ramp for 35 North. Hot chocolate flowed through my icy veins

keeping me alert for a couple of hours, before I exited to Wichita,

Kansas and fell back asleep, this time in a Starbuck's parking lot, but

only for a few hours, until black crows paced back and forth on the

roof of my car, waking me up to the rising eastern sun. There was a

Walmart behind the Starbucks – a good time for another oil and filter

change and tire rotation. I left my car with a friendly black-face, in

his fifties, and made my way on foot to the coffee shop, where I

ordered a pumpkin spice latte and a slice of banana nut bread. I was happy this morning, happy to be alive, and happy that I knew deep down inside, I had been the best wife, mother, and teacher that I knew how to be.

I made it to Limon, Kansas by evening. Coldness surrounded me as I nestled down into the driver's seat of my car under my blankets. I tried not to think about it, closing my eyes to the Phillip's 66 neon light that glowed red behind me. *Sleep.* I told myself. *Just sleep.* It must have worked, as five hours passed, before I pulled the lever, adjusting my seat to the upright position once again. It was only four-thirty in the morning, too dark for travel, but I promised myself I would be extra cautious. *Just an hour.* That's when I stopped for oatmeal at a McDonalds and fell asleep for a couple more hours in their parking lot. *Shift-sleeping.* I thought.

It had been a long haul since leaving Asheville, and my emotions were running high, leaving me drained. I was tired when I entered Denver, Colorado, but I knew I could pull myself together, long enough to walk around the outskirts of Mile High Stadium. Bronco jerseys were on bodies, tailgating in the parking lot, men and women, most with a beer in hand, laughing over the smell of burgers and hotdogs, cooking on grills that seemed to be on every other truck's open tailgate. I smiled at their comradery, a get-together to support the Broncos, over 1,200 miles away in Oakland, an away game, getting ready to take on the Raiders. Their friendships made me yearn for my own, so I made my way back to my car, drove for twenty-minutes, just enough to exit Denver, before stopping at another McDonalds, where I was able to get a large unsweetened ice tea and free internet, the latter connecting me with missed friends. Facebook was something I was still new at, but I enjoyed reading friends' posts, and sharing photos of places I had been visiting. *Fun,* I thought, except for the constant arguing over which person would be best for the next president: Hillary or Donald. A month ago, it was fun reading people's opinions, but recently things had grown hateful. I flipped past the political banter, until I came across stories that were happening locally. That's when I stopped – a breaking news alert caught my eye, as well as the words – *Mile High Stadium,* *explosives,* and *death.* I clicked on the page, hoping for up-to-date details, shaking my head in disbelief that I had just left there.

I silently read the words over and over: *Witnesses say a parking lot trash can exploded. The blast killed ten people at a tailgating party in the Broncos' Sports Authority Mile High Stadium.*

Police suspect explosives may have been involved. ATF and the local bomb squad unit are on the scene.

I felt like tragedy had followed me on my journey, no matter which state, no matter which month. Endless. I signed off Facebook, made my way back to the highway, and drove. While studying my rearview mirror, I thought of the eight people who had lost their lives, the friendships cut short, and the families that had been broken; then I watched the golden hills follow me, as I crossed into Wyoming. I stopped when I got to the Four Plains Motel. Room 10. I didn't want to be cold tonight.

Chapter Twenty-One

Douglas Brandt, a man who was forced to leave his condemned

home in Wichita, Kansas, has been arrested for allegedly placing

thirty-pounds of explosives, in the bottom of a parking lot trash can,

on property belonging to the Broncos' Sports Authority Mile High

Stadium. A bomb squad unit that investigated the scene, speculates

that a fan tossed an empty beer bottle in the can, which caused the

explosives to ignite, destroying six vehicles in the immediate area,

and resulting in ten deaths – six men, three women, and one eleven-

year-old boy. Enola reviewed the news in her head before shutting off the small television in her motel room, and heading out. *The Broncos lost by ten points to the Oakland Raiders. They also lost ten fans. Innocent lives taken for no reason. Pure evil.*

The November weather was perfect for windows down and seventy-five mph on 25 North, just enough of a chill to take Enola's mind off the fans that died for no reason. *Focus.* She reminded herself, as she made her way to her new home – Washington State. She didn't stop to stretch her legs until Kaycee, Wyoming, where she started a friendly conversation with two young men getting gas at a Sinclair station off Mayoworth Road.

"Those are big deer." Enola was referring to the two large creatures, both dead, tied to the back of their tailgate.

"They're antelope." A camouflaged thirty-something voice spoke proudly.

"Did you use a bow and arrow or a gun?" Enola questioned the young man.

"We each used rifles this morning." He answered her inquisitive eyes that were studying him, eyes that tried to understand what behaviors separate animals from mankind.

"Then we retrieve them using the four-wheel." The taller hunting partner spoke up. He was looking at Enola, trying to figure out if she was judging their actions.

Enola turned slightly to address him. "Are antelope good to eat?" She questioned, wondering if they did it for sport, food, or both.

"Yes." He answered, even though he had decided she *was* making judgments. "I see you're from Florida." He looked past Enola to the rear of her car. "Have you eaten Alligator?" He questioned.

"Yes." She replied. "Lots of times." Enola knew he had made his point without much effort. She smiled at both of the men, realizing that people who hunt for food, are still within the moral compass. "It's good."

"Does it taste like chicken?" The first man grabbed Enola's attention back, unaware that the conversation had been about good versus bad actions.

"Yes." They all laughed, accepting each other's lifestyle choices. "Take care." She smiled at them, before stealing one more glance of the man who had looked deeper inside of her, evaluating her inquisitiveness.

"You too." They both echoed.

And then, "Have a safe trip back to Florida." The taller man said.

Enola didn't correct him. She didn't want him to be capable of seeing through her, not a second time, so she didn't explain that she wouldn't be going back anytime soon, if ever again. She smiled at the fact that she was just as camouflaged as they were behind her tinted windows and hidden Rubbermaid containers. She got in her car and drove – windows down.

She reached Montana by three in the afternoon, was tired, but wanted to stop somewhere so she could eat, explore, and sleep. She set her cruise control on seventy-five, stopping only for an occasional restroom break, before finally maneuvering onto 90 West, to Billings, Montana. Starving, she made her way to the only restaurant that caught her attention, one she had first noticed advertised on a billboard several miles back – Famous Dave's Barbecue off King Avenue. She studied the menu, thinking about antelope and camouflage, before choosing a plate of pulled pork with coleslaw and potato salad.

The food was delicious, the service great, and Enola left with a full stomach as she made her way down the street to Ross Department Store. She studied the odd furniture pieces in the back corner of the store, wondering what her new apartment would look like a month from now, after having a few weeks to get settled in. She smiled thinking about how she could reinvent herself – furniture, themes, dishes, bathroom towels, a shower curtain, and even new clothes and boots. *A new hair color?* She wondered as she had already grown tired of the mahogany. *Shorter?* She questioned, even though she had three inches removed the last time she got it cut.

Leaving Ross empty-handed, purely because of having very little room in the car, more than anything else, she drove a few miles down the road to a coffee shop and ordered a chai tea latte. She sat by the window, sipping the warmth, and watching the Montana sun dip into the ground. She didn't panic when darkness moved in quickly, as she had already noticed a Walmart in town – her hiding spot until morning. Staring at the darkness, she wondered what life was going to be like in Washington. She had lived in Florida since being fifteen years old, with the exception of living in Los Angeles, California with Rex, her first husband, and the father of her two children, for a year. Nonetheless, she knew she had been a Florida resident for the best part of thirty-nine years. She was leaving a lifetime behind, *had* left a lifetime behind, and was getting ready to start a new one. She could be anything she wanted. She was starting over. Everything new.

#

Aaron Bosman was distraught over Denver. *Ten lives lost.* Still, he knew he needed to stay focused. There were fifty-five pounds of Asad's explosives still out there, and all he had to go on was Montana and the name Fajar. DMV records didn't show anyone living in Montana with that last name, or the surrounding states for that matter. Associate Deputy Director Bosman had hit a dead end. No way to track the current whereabouts of the remaining fifty-five pounds of explosives. Now it was a game of wait-and-see.

#

I followed 90 West toward my new life, making it as far as I could, before I finally stopped at Little River Motel, in Saint Regis,

Montana. A woman named Linda rented me cottage number eight, a cozy room, with a bed almost as big as the room itself, one that stood boldly when I unlocked the door. Its surface greeted me with a white quilted-spread, displaying a handstitched circle of flowers. Almost unnoticeably, a small television and tiny refrigerator sat quietly in the left corner. And, the bathroom sink, was peculiarly placed near the foot of the bed, the bathroom's size only large enough to accommodate a toilet and shower. The uniqueness made it feel warm. Friendly. I used the bathroom, before moving back near the bed, to give my hands and face attention at the white porcelain sink. Refreshed. Next, I laid out my clothes for morning, grabbed my keys and wallet, and made my way down the street, to a restaurant named Jaspers. After sitting in a corner booth, I ordered an ice tea and Fresno burger with fries, texted Allie to let her know I was only 112 miles from my new apartment, and listened to the locals at Jaspers talk about how life used to be different. I knew the feeling. Life was different – love, marriage, divorce, retirement, and moving to cold country. I tried to put on a brave face as I bit the Fresno. A piece of onion pulled free from the burger and bacon slice. I tucked it back in. I didn't want to lose it. I wanted to taste every part of the sandwich. I wanted to taste my new life. After dinner, I maneuvered my car down a dirt road, visible from the town's only intersection, to a river. I parked, walked over a set of railroad tracks, and stared at the cold flow of water before me. The current and rocks made it hard to see the bottom clearly. It was unknown like the rest of my life, a river of uncertainty. The sound of flowing water carried over, becoming part of my dreams, on a comfortable bed, that my body had missed. Tomorrow, I would arrive in Spokane, my new home.

#

Apartment 307 sat on the top of a steep ravine overlooking three different mountain ranges, gold and red trees danced in the wind, and a train marked *Canadian Railways* carefully maneuvered around the top edge of the first mountain range closest to Enola's balcony. It was the perfect view. Even more perfect, was the fact that Allie and Reese had driven up from Oregon, a surprise they had been working on for days, to help Enola move her containers upstairs and go shopping for a bed, desk, some shelving, and a few things for the kitchen.

Enola didn't let go of Allie's hand as they entered the apartment for the first time. Reese and the rental administrator from the leasing office followed behind. Enola had been happily surprised, after settling into a Walmart parking lot the evening prior, about ten miles from the apartment, when Allie and Reese came up behind her. She had guessed Allie was driving toward Spokane, heard the air racing outside Allie's driver's window each time they chatted on the phone, and sensed Allie was making her way closer, when she asked about where Enola would be sleeping the last evening without an apartment. *Which Walmart Mom?* Enola recalled. That was when Enola smiled. Secretively. Without ruining the surprise that she hoped she was right about. Now, she had everything she wanted: a beautiful view, a cozy studio apartment with a large bathroom and walk-in shower, plenty of closets and cabinets, a cute kitchen with all black appliances and a granite counter, and Allie's presence. She smiled at the first week of November from the balcony, shook the rental administrator's hand, and reached for her key. It was done.

Allie and Reese worked endlessly with Enola, carrying Rubbermaid containers up three flights of stairs, hauling up several

Walmart purchases that Enola had managed to squeeze in her car the evening prior, and finally, leaving Enola's car free of clutter, like it had been when she pulled it off the car lot three years ago. Allie and Enola filled oak-stained cabinets with dishes, organized the bathroom closet with neatly folded towels, and hung all of Enola's clothes on matching plastic blue hangers, another middle of the night purchase, while Reese opened and assembled furniture from factory stapled boxes: a new desk for Enola's laptop, a black entertainment center, and a 28" television with Roku. Allie helped Enola decide what items were still needed: bathroom rugs and trash can, kitchen rug to match her pepper bottles, an outside doormat, some sort of a bed, and a cheap three or four-drawer dresser.

Tuesday turned to Thursday before Enola knew it, and the apartment had become a home: showers had been taken, pasta had been eaten, television had been watched, laundry had been done, floors had been swept, carpets had been vacuumed, and empty Rubbermaid containers had been passed down to Allie and Reese so they could better organize their new home: a pull-behind camper that they had acquired in Oregon. Another surprise, and one that Enola was happy about. She didn't like the thought of her daughter living in a car. Now, she felt a little better, knowing that Allie and Reese had somewhere to stretch out, a place where their dogs fought for position at one end, and a place where they had made a comfortable bed for themselves at the other end. It's a start. Enola knew.

"Thanks for letting us do all our laundry and take showers here," Allie said.

"Anytime," Enola replied, trying not to cry at the thought of them leaving. "Do you have to go so soon?"

"Yes, we've got jobs to get back to." She smiled but was also fighting tears. "We're going to need a different car to pull that camper, even though it's lightweight." Allie followed up. "We'll try to come back in a couple weeks, for Thanksgiving." She added.

They stood there, talking about transmissions, talking about Allie and Reese's new jobs, at a TA travel center: Reese pumping gas, Allie cashiering. Another surprise. Legit jobs. Enola touched Allie's hand, before pulling her close, the warmth of her skin against her mother's face, conversations cut short because of responsibilities. Enola knew they had one day to make it back to their lives. *Work tomorrow.* She remembered.

"I'll miss you Allie." She wanted her to stay, become little again, so they could start over. "Reese, take care of her for me." She asked lightly, but wasn't kidding.

"I will." He answered, before Allie, her emotions still searching for words to respond to her mother.

"You mean the world to me, Mom." Allied formed what she wanted to say. "I love you." She hugged her mom, then bravely turned away.

"I love you too," Enola said to the back of her daughter, no longer a child, but a grown woman. "I love you both." Her conversation followed them down the three flights of stairs. First Allie and Shiloh, then Reese and Zeus. She wanted to scream *come back*, but her voice was upstaged by another train, this one marked *BNSF* – The Burlington Northern Santa Fe Railroad. She pictured endless miles of train track stretching from coast to coast, a symbol that represented her life.

Chapter Twenty-Two

Enola May Starks felt like a fish out of water, and it wasn't until she

had driven Division Street at least six times, that she finally started

to know her way around downtown Spokane. What she didn't know,

was that she had driven by Abdul Fajar Artan, a refugee from

Somali, a legal resident of the U.S., a pharmaceutical student at

Washington State University, two different times.

Two weeks passed quickly for Enola, a stroll through North

Town Mall, a routine dental appointment, a new driver's license, and several grocery shopping trips, carefully choosing from a smorgasbord of food stores – Safeway, Fred Meyer, Yokes, and Rosauers – where her recent objective had been to gather food needed for Thanksgiving, a day that was upon her, and one she was excited about, as she knew Allie and Reese had left for Spokane early that morning, and would be arriving within the next two hours. Enola had a twenty-pound turkey in the oven, crammed with homemade bread and celery stuffing, Waldorf-salad in the frig, a tray of deviled eggs, and celery sticks that looked like caterpillars (crème cheese torsos with blackberry heads and candy eyes), which seemed to stare out at her every time she opened the refrigerator. She heard the sound of anxious dogs moving up the stairwell, just outside her door, and opened her door to Allie and Reese's smiles, before either one could knock. Hugs were exchanged, long and hard, and tears touched Enola's cheeks, this time out of joy. They picked up where they last left off – good conversation, laughter, and huddling around the heat from the oven, in an attempt to offset the thirty-eight-degree chill that had followed them inside. It felt like Thanksgiving. The only missing component was Mitch. Enola had tried to figure out which cargo ships left New York the day she last spoke with him, but there were endless, and she quickly realized she had no way to get in contact with him. Allie knew he was on her mother's mind. She missed him too, her brother, the one that had protected her against bullies, and the one that helped her understand that family was important; now, he was away from family. His only focus was himself.

By two in the afternoon, Reese was mashing potatoes, and Enola and Allie were monitoring the temperature of the turkey-gravy, while wrapping bacon and pastry dough in alternating twists around stems of asparagus, the last thing to go in the oven. By three, all the food was ready, and was carefully placed on a squatty walnut coffee table, that Enola had picked up at a garage sale, a couple days back. That's when Enola realized she had enough food to feed ten people, a fact that became more obvious, as the three of them lowered themselves to the floor, sitting with their backs against the wall, and eyes level with the top of the Thanksgiving spread. Chairs were something Enola hadn't acquired.

"Everything looks great, Enola." Reese always used her first name.

"I'm so glad you guys are here." She smiled, wider, after feeling Allie's grip on her right hand. Squeeze.

"I love you so much Mom," Allie said before letting go and devouring a piece of hot turkey.

"I love you too." Enola looked at her brown eyes. They were eyes that would always remind her of Rex. Allie would always be a part of him. Just like Mitch – a look-alike for Rex's build and nose. There was no escaping the fact that they were his kids. There was no forgetting the fact that Enola and Rex had once loved each other, even though Rex would never admit it now.

Shiloh and Zeus waited patiently, sprawled out on the carpet in front of the glass sliding door, catching the sunrays from the three o'clock sun. They knew their turn would come – a turn for pieces of turkey and scraps of mashed potatoes and stuffing that were left on plates that had seen more than one helping.

Allie and Reese had to leave early Saturday, to make the three-hundred-mile trip back to Aurora, Oregon, back to more paychecks, like the ones that had helped them purchase a used Chevy Tahoe over the last two weeks, a vehicle that handled pulling a small trailer much easier than the Dodge Neon.

"Please drive carefully." Enola fought back tears. It didn't matter that Allie was only three-hundred-miles away, and it didn't matter that she had seen her twice in the month of November. What mattered was that Enola was emotionally exhausted from fighting fear all her life: first as a child, then as a single mother, and now, coming to terms with the fact that she and those she loved were brightly painted bullseyes, in a world of violent extremists. The last five months on the road had heightened Enola's awareness; she knew that people were moving targets, animals waiting to be hunted, victims of illegal sport. She didn't want Allie to become another number.

"Don't worry, Mom." The brown eyes said to her. "We will figure out how to see each other on Christmas." The same brown eyes smiled.

"I love you." Enola tried to stay strong. "Please call me when you get back to Oregon."

"I will," Allie said as she went in for one last hug. "I promise."

\#

Aaron Bosman was yelling at the top of his lungs. "It's the fucking

middle name!" He shuffled through piles of investigative inquiries, a

stack of every Fajar that he could find in the United States, hundreds

now scattered on the top of his mahogany-stained desk, before

locating the one he had spent the morning looking at, and then

quickly handing the crinkled 8 x 11 sheet of paper to one of his field

agents. The name **Abdul Fajar Artan**, in a medium font-size,

headed the paper. Within minutes, a nearby agent was running the

name through several major databases. *From Montana.* HIT.

Pharmaceutical student at WSU in Spokane. The word *Montana*

made Associate Deputy Director Bosman's head spin. *Got him.* He

thought. Then, *where are my explosives?*

#

Manito Park had several weeping willow trees, each with long

strands of golden leaves, that danced in the wind, the perfect setting

for the mallard, its brown wings tilted at an angle, allowing me to

take notice of the brightly colored blue plumage that stretched closer

to its body. My movement sent the seven or eight ducks up into the

December air, forming a loose *V*.

I watched them fly, until they became tiny black dots in the distant sky, before getting in my car, and making my way down Division Street, the road littered with icy patches from the night before, and roofs sprinkled with snow-flurries, a Hansel and Gretel storybook, where I imagined fluffy white pieces of cotton candy in place of shingles. A collection of flashing blue and red lights stood out against the winter sky, prompting my mind to return to reality, and replacing the Hansel and Gretel fairy tale with a scene from the *Cops* TV show. No longer was there a candied house surrounded by a magical forest. Now, there were three patrol cars blocking Division Street, and another two, blocking the road that ran down the middle of Washington State University property. My car sat still, as directed, the woodcutter and his domestic wife were characters replaced with police officers – guns drawn. A part of me wanted to back up, not wishing to witness anything that was about to happen, but I was boxed in, unable to move, even after hearing the sound of distant gunshots. The sound, life-taking, made me think of Allie and Mitch, wishing for their safety in a world gone mad. I had just talked to Allie yesterday, confirming that I would travel to Oregon for Christmas, and that she would be working when I arrived, but only for another hour or two, long enough for me to grab coffee, anything to keep my mind off of my missing son. She hated as much as I did, that her brother's whereabouts were still unknown, and she hated that another holiday would be celebrated without him, not even a phone call, just long enough to say hello. I remembered his hurried voice calling from New York. Rushed. *I love you too Ma.* Then, after using any available time he had left to talk, he seemed to disappear, right in the middle of *keep the same phone number* and *let Allie know that I love her*. I wanted to hear his voice, but all I could do was think of him. There were no missed calls. Something I checked for every day.

Now, after several gunshots, I sat rattled under the gray December sky. Tomorrow, I would leave for Oregon.

Chapter Twenty-Three

The Alcohol, Tobacco, and Firearms division in Detroit should have

been celebrating. Abdul Fajar Artan had been shot and killed by

police in Spokane, Washington. The problem was, a big fucking

problem to say the least, the explosives were not in his possession, or

in the apartment off Boone that agents had taken so long to locate, an

apartment that had been rented under a former roommate's name.

Now, there was no one to question. Abdul Fajar Artan was dead. The

roommate was in another state. And the explosives were not there.

Where were they? Bosman was fuming, fifty-five pounds of explosives, vanished. He wanted someone to blame, but he knew the Spokane police had done their job, knew Abdul had been shot as a last resort, after he failed to comply with the very loud, and very clear instructions given. *Drop your weapon.* Bosman read the report. He knew that it was either a cop's life or Artan's, still he wished he could interrogate the stupid son-of-a-bitch. *Where did you put the explosives asshole?*

#

Enola May combed her hair straight back, letting it fall in any direction it favored, before deciding to gather it together, forming one ponytail, now that it had grown longer, and then used a scrunch-tie to gather it to the middle of her head in back, about three inches from the base of her neck, an area that felt sensitive when touched; although, being touched in her sensitive areas was something she had put on the back burner, no longer trying to find someone to be with, and content in the fact that she might spend the rest of her life alone. It was a chance to be herself, and sporting a mixture of silver, brunette, and faded mahogany at her temples, was something she wore proudly. It was time to refamiliarize herself with the face that had earned laugh lines, frown lines, and permanent indentations. Like the Grand Canyon, Enola's face had reshaped itself over the years. She knew her chin used to be more defined. Even so, she looked beautiful; although, she never thought of herself as anything but average.

Arriving Christmas Eve, Enola pulled her Hyundai next to their Chevy Tahoe and camper. Allie and Reese were notified when she parked, even though quietly, by Shiloh and Zeus, both with hearing that focused on every little sound. But the barking ceased, as soon as they laid eyes on Enola, treats in hand, and the familiar smell of a woman they knew was part of the family.

"Merry Christmas Eve." Allie's faced gleamed. "I guess my directions were good." She concluded.

"Yes, they were." Enola smiled. "Merry Christmas Eve." She said back.

"Merry Christmas Eve." A third time. This time from Reese, who was ordering Shiloh and Zeus away from the camper door, so Enola could step in.

Hugs were exchanged, and a round of hot chocolate was passed out, while Reese showed Enola additions they had added to the small pull camper: a propane cook stove, a bed frame for their mattress, giving them extra support and lifting it off the floor, so they could sit comfortably throughout the day, two dog beds at the other end of the camper, and a well-organized supply of canned goods and other non-perishables in the cabinet across the front. Allie was the one to point out the large blue and white ice chest in the middle of the camper, its height matching the small black table, whose surface accommodated the propane cook stove. Their smiles matched their lifestyle: free, uninhibited, and sincere. They didn't need riches to be happy, weren't prisoners of bureaucracy, and made their own way in life.

Reese liked to cook, so the evening was met with a large pan of pasta and shrimp, a colorful display that even Gordon Ramsay would be proud of, perfectly seasoned, with green and red bell peppers, and small bits of spicy sausage. It was delicious, and the moments they spent together were even more succulent. Tender glances were exchanged, and unrestrained conversation flowed in the small camper, until one day ended and the next began. That's when Enola stretched out in her three-year-old Hyundai the best she could, even though the back-passenger seats had been securely put back in place, and the futon had been discarded thousands of miles ago. Enola managed to make do with the two large pillows and four blankets; some worked as padding and some worked as coverage. At least the temperatures didn't go much below forty, not like the lower twenties that she had left in Spokane.

Christmas Day, Enola gave Shiloh and Zeus new dog bones, large rawhides that challenged them for hours, and Allie and Reese were presented with a collection of spices, oven mitts, two new cooking pans, and some clothes for each – all things Enola had heard them mention over the last month on the phone. Enola wasn't expecting anything, but her face lit up when she opened several wrapped boxes: a tabletop makeup mirror, several fizzy bath bombs, and a pair of warm slippers. Apparently, Enola wasn't the only one that paid attention on the phone.

The day flowed, with more conversation, lots of laughter, ham steaks with mashed potatoes and peas, and the graciousness that swelled both inside and outside of that small camper, for the here and now, and for each breath. Enola thought of Mitch, wondered why he wasn't calling. She also thought of Dixie, reaching for her phone, to make a quick phone call, but then realized her lifelong friend had already sent a text, an hour back: *Merry Christmas, Nola. I know you went to Oregon to see the kids, but I wanted to wish you a great day. I love you, Sis.*

Enola texted back, thinking about how Allie and Reese were still young. *Kids.* She reviewed the word, and settled on the fact that they were, compared to fifty-five-year-olds. The thought made Enola smile, as she pressed send: *Merry Christmas Sis. I love you so much. Please give a big hug to Ryan. I'll head back to Spokane in the morning.* She knew Allie and Dixie would always be in her life. Still she yearned for her adult son. Christmas without hearing from him was hard. She closed her eyes, stealing a moment of serenity.

Morning came early, but Enola knew the drive back was going to be slower than usual and wanted to get an early start, especially after getting an alert on her phone that several mountain passes had been hammered in the middle of the night with ice and snow. Nonetheless, goodbyes weren't something she was good at. After knocking, and waiting for Allie's invitation to enter, Enola pulled open the camper door and met Shiloh's black mound of long hair and dark eyes, both of which followed her to the edge of Allie

and Reese's bed, where Enola settled into a sitting position next to

Allie, her daughter, and her proof that generational abuse can be

replaced with love and tenderness. Enola studied her younger

version, without speaking, smiling at the French-Irish button nose

that had been passed down from Melantha. *Some things can't be*

replaced. She thought, as a tear made its way down her cheek, but

was captured by Shiloh's careful lick, a combination of sincerity and

excitement. Zeus sat, waiting his turn. His box-shaped jawline

forwarded an appearance of force, but came close to Enola with the

gentleness of a clawless kitten. His strong muscular neck squared off

at the top of Enola's shoulders, as his long pink tongue licked

Enola's face, capturing another tear. She hugged him back, his pit

bull inheritance, making him a target for judgment. Now, that most

of the tears had been licked away, Enola attempted to speak without

shedding more.

"I'll miss you." She said, knowing that it would probably be

summer before they saw each other again. "You're my best

Christmas present," Enola added.

"I'm so glad you drove down to see us," Allie said, also fighting tears. "I love you Mom." Her look matched Enola's thoughts – *goodbyes never get easier.* "Being with you is Christmas." Her words pulled at Enola's heartstrings and reactivated a whole new stream of tears, hidden by a mixture of jawline kisses and hugs, before Enola finally made her way to her vehicle, and slowly pulled away. She could see Zeus in her rearview, his defensive posture standing guard outside their camper, a victim of his hereditary genes, an easy target for profiling, but then in her next thought, she imagined everyone is from time to time.

#

The Spokane community was divided about the death of Abdul Fajar Artan. Witnesses said he had a gun when he exited the pharmaceutical building at WSU. Police had ordered him several times to put down his weapon. He didn't comply. At first, it seemed an open and shut case. The only complication, at least in Associate Deputy Director Bosman's opinion, was the missing explosives. Now, additional details had surfaced, surrounding the day before Christmas Eve, the day a twenty-four-year-old WSU student met his God. First, Abdul Fajar Artan was born in Billings, Montana.

Second, he moved to Spokane, after receiving a scholarship at WSU,

and third, he fought against radical Muslims, and most importantly,

the weapon spotted in his hand by several witnesses and the officer

who shot him, was an 8GB digital sound audio recorder, that Abdul

used to record lectures.

#

It wasn't until another week had passed, a new year, 2017, that

Bosman had located another man with the name of Fajar. This time

it served as a first name. He tried to feel confident, knowing the man

was associated with the state of Montana, this time Missoula, a city

that had less than one percent Muslims, and a city that the new

suspect had recently left. *Did he have the explosives?* Associate

Deputy Director Bosman questioned. He knew his confidence had

hit an all-time low, as he second-guessed the phone-call he had made

to Spokane police department prior to the December incident, just to

inform them that they had a possible suspect in their area, a student

at WSU. He wished they would have taken it as information only, as

intended, and as instructed, instead of cornering the twenty-four-

year-old student. *Was Abdul's death partially my fault?* He

questioned, before regaining his composure and calling in several of his agents for a brief meeting. This time the topic was – Fajar ibn Wayne, current whereabouts unknown.

#

Enola called Dixie, just before eight in the morning, almost eleven North Carolina time, to make sure her lifelong friend knew she was thought of.

"Happy Birthday Sis," Enola said the words to the hello she recognized. It was Dixie. Someone that had been part of her life since first grade.

"Thanks Nola." She smiled, her cheek pressed against the phone. "I'm glad you caught me." She sounded excited. "Ryan's taking me to Pigeon Forge for my birthday." Enola knew that was one of Dixie's favorite places.

"I'm so happy for you," Enola said. "I just wanted to call and say Happy Birthday and let you know I was thinking about you." She had sent a card about five days ago, before holding herself captive in her apartment for a few days, to catch up on some laundry and housework, before another road trip, this one only three hours.

"I got your card and chocolate bar this morning." Dixie was grabbing her last-minute items and struggling to lock the front door with her free hand. "Blueberry chocolate bar," Dixie announced. "Made in Leavenworth." She had taken notice. "I hope it doesn't have calories." She laughed.

"It doesn't Dix," Enola answered, thinking about of her recent day trip to Leavenworth, three hours northwest from Spokane, a quaint little Bavarian town, loaded with gift shops, a day she spent having a Bratwurst at München Haus' Grill, and several hours later, an evening Spätzle at the Bavarian Bistro and Bar. She could still remember the taste of the tiny noodle-shaped dumplings, each bite she painstakingly matched up with a piece of beef from the Hungarian goulash. Enola pulled herself back to the here-and-now and away from the rich sauce flavored with bacon, onion, and garlic. "Go and enjoy yourself Sis." She said into the phone. "I love you."

"Okay, Nola." Dixie Durrant answered. "I love you too, Sis." Enola hung up the phone, already eleven days into the New Year. She still hadn't heard from Mitch. Four months. *Was he unable to make a call from the cargo ship?* She wondered. The feeling of an incurable absence filled her, something she had felt many times in her life, a hunger that was ignored. She had felt it growing inside of her, since Christmas had passed, since Mitch still hadn't called, since the snow had fallen over the last week, hard, and since the Spokane

temperatures had reached negative numbers. Being a Spokanite,

wasn't for the weak.

Chapter Twenty-Four

Fajar ibn Wayne was thirty-one years old, had served six years for

armed robbery, and was American as apple pie. Warden Davy at the

Montana prison said he remembered Fajar, distinctly, and that other

Muslims referred to the man as a revert, someone that converted to

Muslim from another religion.

"Muslims believe every human being meets Allah before

birth." Bosman heard the controlled chuckle underneath Warden

Davy's statement. "They believe all people are born Muslim." He continued, this time accompanied by a loud belly laugh. "I can tell you this much Director Bosman, I ain't never been Muslim." His laugh bounced around in Bosman's head, as much as the information he spilled from the prisoner's file – *Born: Donald Jay Davis. Father: Wayne Tanner Davis. Mother: deceased. Reverted to Muslim while serving six years for armed robbery. Chose the name Fajar to honor his Muslim faith.*

"I appreciate the information." Bosman kept humor out of his voice. All business.

"They're protected ya know." Davy followed up Bosman's acknowledgment with more information. "The fucking constitution protects 'em." Davy sounded exceptionally pissed off as he continued to ramble. "I had to change his name from Donald to Fajar on all his records." He sighed. "Plus, the crazy bastard gets to have ibn as his middle name and his father's first name as his last." He laughed again. "It's a right, ya know?" Warden Davy asked, but it was clearly an announcement.

"What is the meaning of ibn?" Bosman asked, hoping to avoid more small talk, but wanting an answer.

"Are you ready for this?" Another question that was the precursor to more information. "It means *son of*."

"Thanks Warden Davy." Aaron Bosman hung up the phone, quickly, before Davy stopped laughing; his immediate concern was one thing, and one thing only. *Where is Fajar ibn Wayne?* His mind searched for answers, and he wasn't going to rest until Fajar, aka, Donald was sitting in front of him.

#

February 11, 2017 a United States commercial cargo ship near Somali, was boarded by ten armed men. Pirates. There wasn't time for a distress call from the captain's quarters. The Puntland Maritime Police Force is now involved. No other details are known at this time.

Enola could hardly breathe after hearing the news report on her small television. She had no idea which ship her son worked on, whether the ship on the news could be the one he boarded in New York, or whether there were any injuries in the incident. *No other details are known at this time.* She played the last piece of the report over and over in her head. *What did that mean?* She questioned. She desperately wanted to hear Mitch's voice. *Is my son okay?* She sat frozen, staring out her glass sliding door at the February snow, hoping for a miracle, a sign that he was safe. A faded cardinal landed in a tall pine adjacent to the top railing of her third-floor balcony. It wasn't enough. She needed more. First, she would call the local news station and insist on speaking with a reporter. Someone, somewhere, would have a list of the American workers on that ship. She needed to know if Mitch's name was on the list. She began to dial.

Enola wanted to cry, and did, every day, until she wasn't able to cry anymore, her eyes dry, focused on the BNSF train that roared past, the track only half a football field away from her glass sliding door, making its way through snow and thick gray mist. She thought of Mitch, her son, who, like the train, was in charge of his path and his speed. She knew it would be a while before she heard from him again. She reviewed the findings after several days of calling. First the news station, then the cargo ship company, then the U.S. embassy in Mogadishu, the capital. They had checked him in, offered him a room at the nearest hotel with other members of the crew, all of which had been rescued unharmed, and all of which would be re-boarding the cargo ship to continue to other ports, but

Mitch Narducci had refused, taking his pay, and leaving the security

of the embassy. He simply walked away, commenting to the U.S.

official that he would like to *stay awhile* and that *living somewhere*

for less than two dollars a day was what he needed right now. His

mother found the news heartbreaking. He could have called from the

embassy to his family in the U.S. like all the other crew members,

but he didn't. He was gone, exercising his right to stay in Somali.

What do you mean by his right? Enola recalled her teary-eyed

question to the official. Then she recalled his answer. Short.

Detached. It wasn't his son. *He has a passport, so he can easily stay*

six months, ma'am.

Spokane, Washington could be a reminder of how cold life

can be. It's constant chill, temperatures in the twenties throughout

the last several days poked at Enola like bits of her past. She walked

down three flights of stairs, careful to avoid ice that seems glued in

place, watching her every step to the silver mailboxes that were cold

to the touch without a gloved hand. She pulled several pieces of mail

from the box: a booklet of classes offered at the local recreational

center, and a letter from Allie with a general delivery address. She

smiled recognizing Allie's left-handed print. She had just talked to

Allie a few days ago, to inform her about the cargo ship, to inform

her that her brother was safe, and then, in just a few words, she tried

to inform her how he simply walked away, without calling his

mother or sister. *There's nothing you can do Mom.* Enola could still

hear her daughter's wisdom. *It was his decision.* And then, *I'm*

sending you something. Keep a lookout. Enola recalled bits and

pieces of their conversation, as she removed her gloves and carefully

ripped open the top of the envelope. She was glad the tear was

gentle, without much damage to the envelope, after noticing that

Allie had written *Gvgeyui Forever Mom* along the inside flap. She

pulled the letter out slowly. It was simple, a white envelope, and a

piece of lined notebook paper inside that looked like it had been torn

from a spiral pad, yet it was everything Enola needed – *Here's a*

coupon for a free haircut. We won't use it, and I know there's a few

of these salons up by you. I love you Mom. Don't ever forget that.

You are a good mom. You didn't do anything wrong. People are who

they are. Enola focused on the last sentence. Maybe she didn't know

who her son was, not anymore.

A tear rolled down Enola's face which she wiped away with

her cold bare hand before heading to her car. It was time to face the

Spokane winter head-on. She thumbed through the parks and

recreation magazine, still in her other hand, while the car's engine

warmed to a slow idle, and frosted car windows cleared. *Yoga.* She

thought. *And maybe a hiking day.* She placed the catalog in the

passenger's seat before pulling on her seatbelt, but only after

promising herself she would stop and register at the center for a

couple of activities. There was no reason not to stop and every

reason to stop. Enola knew she had to be stronger than the weather

and isolation that fought to make her weaker. She knew she could do

better, and by time she pulled away from the parks and recreation

parking lot off Division Street, she felt like she was gaining strength

on the cruel winter sky. Yoga would start in one more week, and the

four-mile hiking trip, that she had also registered for, was scheduled

five days into April, something to look forward to, and a way to

meet new friends. She felt comfortable with her new plan, as she

ended the day by sipping a chai tea latte at a neighborhood coffee

shop, and staring out at the falling snow with a welcoming grin. *I've*

survived too much to let weather beat me. And then, the thought that

plagued her. *Please call me Mitch.* And, *I love you.* Her last thought would always be within reach, even as the snow fought the bottom of her Hyundai, on her way back to her small apartment.

#

Fajar wasn't talking. Even with several agents in his face, and even after the rough treatment he had received, as he was taken into custody. Associate Deputy Director Bosman had flown out to Seattle immediately with a few of his field agents, and he had given strict instructions over the phone. *Don't question him.* The Seattle office held him as instructed; however, their drummed-up version of domestic violence wasn't going to keep him past the routine twenty-hour hold, and the probable cause was a stretch. Fajar's girlfriend was already pacing inside, near the police station's front desk, screaming about how Fajar ibn Wayne hadn't hit her. Associate Deputy Director Bosman didn't care about whether there was PC or not; he only cared about his missing explosives. Still, the desk sergeant was being a constant pain in the ass, reminding Bosman and his men that the clock was ticking before his station would have to release Fajar.

#

It seemed the more it snowed, the stronger Enola got, probably out of spite. The end of February, seemed brighter, a snow-filled-moon illuminated the black sky, and the crisp night filled her lungs. She refused to keep caged, like an animal, taking two-hour hikes in ten inches of snow, going out to dinner with a woman she had met in yoga, and planning occasional weekend getaways. A part of her had always wanted to go to Edmonton, Canada, to see the mall that claimed it was bigger than The Mall of America in Minnesota, a memory that Enola still treasured, five days with Allie, during her eleventh-grade year, shopping in the four-story mall for several days, exploring downtown Minneapolis, and going to the Minnesota Zoo in Apple Valley – where their agreed-upon favorite exhibit was the brown bear. They had stood, looking at the largest grizzly, his size intimidating, his face elongated by the added golden hairs that seemed to drop from his chin, and his eyes fixated on the both of them. Enola knew the moat and thick acrylic were all that separated them from becoming a meal; nonetheless, it was an animal that demanded respect, with its humped shoulders and long straight claws.

#

Fajar ibn Wayne demanded respect too. And, no matter how much it burned Associate Deputy Director Bosman, he had to release the piece of shit after holding him for twenty-four hours. That was several weeks ago. Several weeks of his men staying behind to tail his every move. Several weeks of expense. Several weeks of around the clock surveillance. And, several weeks of nothing. Aaron Bosman shouldn't have been so easy to read. Being in the pen for six years, made Fajar an expert on human emotions. He didn't say one word during the interrogation with Bosman. He let Bosman's emotions do all the talking. *I know you've got my last fifty-five pounds of explosives Donald.* Not only did he remember making the accusation, but he also remembered Donald's smirk. The thought of having the last take from the CSX robbery made Fajar smile from the inside. Now, the game had become more fun. He would blow up several targets. A few pounds at a time. Still, he didn't have a specific target in mind, not until he met Bosman's overanxious eyes, causing his own to glance downward, toward the table in the interrogation room. That's when he decided his target, after noticing the Associate Deputy Director's keyring – a round metal disc dangled from a short silver chain, the disc shaped like a quarter, the background white, with a thick red line that formed a complete circle in the foreground, and a large red line that diagonally stretched from the bottom left to the upper right, a universal signal for NO, a tiny blood transfusion bag appeared behind the diagonal line. He read the tiny words silently and without being noticed, his uncuffed hands directing Bosman's attention elsewhere. The words: *No Blood.* And, *Legal Document in Wallet,* were clearly visible. Now, the fifth of March, Aaron Bosman was on a flight back to Seattle. He was sure the three explosions were Fajar's work, and it was his own damn fault. He had slipped up – again.

Chapter Twenty-Five

Enola made her way, about thirty-five minutes over to the Idaho

border, and up 2 North toward Bonner's Ferry, just inside British

Columbia. She allowed her mind to wander as the road twisted and

turned, sometimes shadowing the outline of the Moyie River. It was

somewhere in those miles, after she had made her way to 3 East, that

she got the call from Dixie, her friend of forty-nine years, the one

person she considered a sister, and the only family she had left from

her childhood. It was when she finally came face to face with Mount

Fernie, that Enola pulled over, long enough to let the phone call sink in, recapitulating Dixie's words, over and over again in her mind. *I have stage four melanoma. It has spread to several lymph nodes.* Tears were blocking out the Canadian skyline as Enola attempted to regain her composure, trying to recall details from Dixie's conversation, but she couldn't, only bits and pieces. Just words. *Metastasized.* And then she recalled – *brain scan – waiting on results.* She couldn't remember how the phone call ended, just that Dixie didn't want her to fly there, not now, just wait. *Wait for what?* Enola screamed at the sky. *What the fuck have you done now?* She wiped her eyes using her black leather gloves, gloves that were fighting to keep the mid-forties at bay, gloves that smeared a sisterhood all over her face. *I don't fucking get you!* She cursed at the sky, still unable to drive, still parked on British Columbia's 3 East. She simply sat there and stared at Mount Fernie. Strips of thick frozen snow, flowed down the mountain like white icing, covering everything in its pathway. The sky hung low around it, gray clouds masking its power. Hours passed.

When she was finally able to stop crying, she followed 3 East to Crow's-Nest Pass and by early evening, around five, she was filling up at the Flying J in Nanton, Alberta which had brought her back to 2 North. It seemed the only logical way to deal with uncertainty, at least in Enola's world, was to drive, and so she did. She reached Calgary by six at night, swung into a public lot marked parking authority, and took in the massive size of Calgary. Skyscrapers fought for the highest position, grabbing her attention, pulling her out of her vehicle, absent a coat, her arms dressed in a long-sleeve pullover and lightly padded sleeveless zip-up vest. Enola let the cold air keep her heart beating. *I can't lose Dixie.* She tried fighting back the tears as she walked over a pedestrian-only bridge which took her to a park and river beside the center of the city. The river was frozen over with ice, the banks covered with snow, and the temperature fought to stay at thirty degrees Fahrenheit.

The world seemed cold, once again, probably the moment Enola rejected what was left of her faith. *If you're real, how can you do this to Dixie?* She looked at the sky. Nothing. No answers. No guarantees. And, no explanations. Just nothing. Enola walked back to her red Hyundai feeling defeated. She continued driving. Hard. Over icy roads. Intent on getting there, wherever there was. She stopped when the sky grew dark. Her mind was more exhausted than her body. She checked into room 115 at the Motel 6 in Innisfail, Alberta.

When morning came, still confused, and questioning how the world can be so cruel to good people, Enola drove for a couple more hours before stopping, just in time too, as the sky opened, a continual downpour of snow hit Enola's face and shoulders as she made her way into the Edmonton Mall. Her destination. Taking in the giant pirate ship in the center of the mall, an ice-skating rink filled with large hands holding smaller hands, a large sculpture of a whale's head busting up through the mall floor, and a Chinese supermarket, all seemed to take Enola's mind off Dixie, but only for a few hours. Until she reached her car again. This time it was covered with snow, bringing her attention back to the sky, and back to a God that could hurt good people, an imaginary God, she convinced herself, as she fought the slushy streets and made her way to 16 West. It was dark before she stopped again. This time it was a Super 8 Motel in Hinton, back over the boundary, back in British Columbia, close to Jasper National Park.

She entered the park the following morning, after stopping at a Safeway supermarket on Carmichael Lane, to buy a whole roasted deli chicken and two large bottles of water, and after stopping at Walmart in the same plaza, to purchase a military-style coat. She had finally conceded to the fact that she had left her only two coats at her apartment, and doing without wasn't a choice. The Canadian air bit her skin with its sharp and unrelenting cold. The sunshine and new coat were her lifelines, in a place where nature ruled, and she imagined, would be God's home, if there was a God. Its beauty couldn't be challenged. As she entered the east entrance of the park, her mind was mesmerized by a world of postcard-like portraits – jagged mountains cut the sky like diamonds, frozen plains at their base, and large evergreens reached toward the sky. The area was called Pocahontas, one of strength and beauty, and had earned its name.

The sun hit Enola's face, lighting up her skin, making it appear softer, as it blended perfectly with her recent new hair color – Marilyn Monroe blond. Her new military jacket had an oversized hood, lined with imitation white fur, which kept Enola's new hair color concealed from the temperatures that had dipped low, the mid-twenties, something she felt whenever she pulled over the car, and something she did often, first to hike a trail, then to take more photos, and finally to sit and stare at the park's halfway point – an area where Enola was teased with an assortment of geological features – slopes, solid rock, mounds, hills, cliffs, valleys, a river, and mountains that seemed to rule the universe.

Enola stopped at Yellowhead Pass to eat lunch, sitting on the hood of her red Hyundai, tearing off one leg of the roasted chicken, as she thought about Mitch in Mogadishu, then eating a second leg, while she searched for some logical reason to explain Dixie's cancer, and finally deciding she needed something to believe in, something that would help her get through this part of her life. *Hope.* She looked at the sky, satisfied that she had replaced her doubt with something real, even though it wasn't tangible, she believed in it. *Hope.* She looked deeper into the sky, past several cumulus clouds. *Is that okay?* She asked. *Can I just call you Hope?* She felt a sense of relief inside her stomach, a few moments of peace, without a familiar flutter, without doubt, without emptiness – just peace. She smiled at the sky, imagining it was filled with Hope.

By four-thirty in the afternoon she had made her way across Jasper National Park and had picked up 5 South, since 93 South was closed due to an avalanche, making the way she wanted to go impossible. She would have to miss traveling through Banff National Park. *Another time.* She thought, although slightly disappointed. It wasn't that 5 South wasn't beautiful, it was, but she had her heart set on traveling to Banff, a thought she let go of by time she stopped at the Avola Service Station for gas, beef jerky, and a king cone – vanilla ice cream and caramel swirled on top of a crisp wafer pastry – treats that lasted her until Kamloops, British Columbia. That's when she swung into a small motel, checked in, secured herself in a room overlooking a small pond, before calling Allie to tell her about the mountains in Jasper National Park, and to gently inform her about Aunt Dixie's mountain – a mountain they both agreed she would successfully climb. Allie always had a way of putting her mother's worries at ease, and was able to focus on life's miracles. She listened to Allie's excitement, as she announced Shiloh's pregnancy, and then they exchanged Gvgeyuis, before Enola allowed her eyes to shut in room 211, at the River-land Inn, her thoughts recycling: *Puppies. Mitch. Dixie. Hope. Puppies. Mitch. Dixie. Hope.*

#

I worked my way out of Kamloops taking 5 South, until my GPS, which I had recently reset for Spokane, directed me to 5A South. That's when I noticed it – a fork in the road, a decision, and a bit of humor from the universe, I imagined. I laughed at the sky. 5A South was what I needed to get back to Spokane. 5 South led directly to a city called HOPE. I laughed. *Funny.* I thought as I continued on the road back to Spokane. *Very funny.*

I processed the coincidence, as I drove toward Washington State, and in the direction needed, passing on the opportunity to go see the city named Hope. *It's out there when I need it – Hope.* I smiled as I thought about it. Such a simple concept and one I could believe in.

The border patrol officer questioned me as I entered the USA.

"Drugs?"

"No."

"Weapons?"

"No."

"Reason for your visit to Canada?"

To find God, I mean Hope. I thought but didn't say it out loud. "To go to the Edmonton Mall and Jasper National Park," I answered instead.

"Alone?"

"Yes." I thought about my name spelled backward.

"You live in Spokane now?" He questioned.

"Yes." Short.

"What brings you all the way from Michigan?" He asked, showing off his skill at reading his computer, being able to see my birthplace, a place I left behind when I was six, a place that had devoured my childhood home and childhood hospital.

"I left there when I was a kid." I looked at him. "I'm from Florida." Thinking of the state where I raised two kids. "I retired and moved to Washington."

"Have a nice day." He motioned me through without a reaction to my explanations. Nothing. I drove home, my only stop at Coulee Dam, where I watched the sun melt into the Washington skyline.

#

Bosman was more pissed at himself than anything else. He knew he had triggered the explosions at three different Jehovah Witness Kingdom Halls in and around Seattle, a rookie mistake; his keychain should have been tucked in his suit pants, not on display for Fajar ibn Wayne. He had fucked up. Inexcusable. He should have known that someone who had taken the time to change his name, in the honor of Allah, might be familiar with other religions too. Bosman had carried the keychain for years, just in case of an accident, especially in his line of work. He believed that accepting a blood transfusion was against scripture, against the Jehovah Witness faith, even in a life or death situation. He knew he had made the mistake, the moment Fajar was released from unsuccessful questioning. The only time Fajar ibn Wayne spoke to Aaron Bosman was on his way out the door. *Don't forget your keys, Director.* It was then, when Bosman turned around to grab them, that he felt they had been studied. Now, he knew.

A deliberate fire was set in each one of the Jehovah Witness Halls, and each one had five pounds of explosives, waiting several feet away, just enough time for Fajar to clear the premises, and make his way to safety. The first was in Lacey, Washington, just sixty miles outside of Seattle. The second, in Tumwater, Washington, only seven miles down the road from the first. And the third, while Associate Deputy Director Bosman was in mid-air, was set in Yelm, Washington, an easy forty-minute drive from Tumwater. All three buildings were destroyed. ATF was certain, no more than five pounds were used in each, but it was just enough to create an explosion, keeping firefighters at a distance, all three, burnt to the ground. A part of Bosman, wanted to take matters into his own hands. *Next time he won't get out of an interrogation room alive.* He thought, but then remembered he had more control than that. Besides, he reminded himself, no people were killed. A woman, inside the Tumwater location, received severe burns, when a portion of the roof collapsed, but firefighters arrived in time to pull her to safety. Still, Bosman knew from experience, that the buildings were part of the community, a place where the entire congregation could gather. Fajar ibn Wayne had made it personal.

Chapter Twenty-Six

Enola May Starks tried to keep *HOPE* alive in everything she did:

chatting with Dixie on the phone about her cancer treatments,

keeping in contact with Allie, taking short hikes, and occasional

weekend trips, the next one planned for Seattle. The first Saturday in

April.

She stood near the corner booth in Pike's Market, watching a

young man Mitch's age, toss Alaskan halibut, salmon, and swordfish

onto beds of ice, each landing in a perfectly displayed position.

Another man, neatly arranged a fresh exhibit of crab, shrimp, lobster, and oysters, adding to the overpowering smell of the great Pacific. She inhaled, appreciating the strong odor. The brine constancy made her nostrils flare, and yearn for more; it was not like the reaction her sense of smell had when she toured the underground world of Seattle, an area that used to be Seattle before the Great Fire of 1889, now reduced to putrid tunnels, full of ash and decay. Taking shallow breaths, she worked her way back to street level, before walking several blocks, her eyes searching for a place where her sense of taste could be challenged. *Queen Sheba's Restaurant?* She questioned herself, but went inside without answering, where she allowed her body to rest in a leather-backed chair, and preceded to order. At first, she was hesitant to use her fingers, but noticed other patrons didn't have utensils either, so she neatly fingered the large silver platter that the waitress had sat down before her – injera (wheat bread) and gomen be siga (combination of beef and collard greens). Cautiously nibbling, she kept her mind open to the unfamiliar flavors. *At least the beef is spicy.* She welcomed the taste of onions and peppers. Next, she sampled the injera, which by visual appearance, looked like a flat pancake, but the taste of fermented flour wasn't agreeing with Enola's taste-buds. *Old shoes.* She hated

the comparison her mind was making, and tried a second time to

develop a taste for the spongy texture, but fell short. Still, she was

able to fill her stomach, and left East John Street happy, as she made

her way by foot to a small bed and breakfast for the night.

The next morning, after a cheese and pepper omelet, Enola

pointed her red Hyundai toward the Skagit Valley Tulip Festival

near Mount Vernon. Stopping at Edmond's Beach, Enola watched

the seagulls fly over Puget Sound, part of the interconnected

waterways leading to the Pacific Ocean. She thought about how

everything is connected, like a puzzle. Her thoughts were linking

more than inlets and basins, they were connecting people, places,

and outcomes. *Does it all come down to being in the wrong place at*

the wrong time? She questioned. *Does Dixie have cancer because of*

where she lives or because of DNA? Are people targeted because of

mass hysteria? Are innocent people killed because they are simply in

the wrong place at the wrong time? The questions were still in her

head as she started over Deception Pass Bridge, a structure that

linked Fidalgo and Whidbey Island. *Another connection.* She

laughed, knowing that Melantha was still running things from somewhere. She went over the bridge slowly, staring out her driver's side, at the head of a sea lion. His bristled face looked silver in the early morning sun, as he glided through the cool Pacific blue-green water. His shiny coat played peek-a-boo with the surface, holding Enola's attention, as her car nearly came to a stop, her rearview mirror was absent of other cars. She lowered her side window, allowing her lungs to breathe in deep amounts of air, before slowly making her descent off the bridge.

By two in the afternoon and after sixty more miles, Enola was snapping photos of tulips: first bright yellow, then purple ones that looked like velvet, followed by red ones that looked like the candy-apple nail polish she had seen at Walmart, and finally, burnt orange tulips that raised their heads to the sun. The assortment of color made her feel alive, having had all of her senses tantalized within the last twenty-four hours, her only remaining one, that still needed more attention, was her sense of touch. Making her way to the Hampton Inn and Suites in Burlington, she parked, and checked in, her hands absent of everything except a small purse and lightweight overnight bag, which she opened immediately, after securing herself in room 230. Slipping on a bathing suit, that she hadn't worn in years, she smiled, happy at the fact that it still fit, and grabbed a towel, before sliding her feet into flipflops, and heading downstairs. The indoor pool and jacuzzi, were the combination she needed. First a four-minute soak in the hot jacuzzi, then a fifteen-minute swim in the lukewarm pool, where she repeated several laps from end to end, loosening muscles that had reacted to violent stories about death, her mind reassuring her muscular system that it was no longer under attack. *Relax.* She thought. *Nourish my body. Control my reactions.* Pieces of friendly advice swam with her. She knew life was fragile, knew danger lurked in every city in every state, but also knew she had to stop pinning tragedy on the universe. There wasn't a controlling authority playing Russian roulette. Dixie wasn't targeted, but her mortality had been threatened – just like the families in Nice, France, just like the innocent victims at the nightclub in Florida, and, just like the many others: the investment officers, the consultants, the insurance agents, the banking executives, the engineers, the government employees, the mothers, the fathers, the sisters, the brothers, the children, and the Carla Yellow Birds. Enola let the water swallow her shoulders, her head bobbing just above the surface, along with her thoughts. *Dixie still has a chance to survive.* She rationalized. *She is a fighter.* She crouched down, allowing the top of her head to submerge itself beneath the surface of the water, letting her body find peace, before emerging anew.

#

Donald Jay Davis walked into the small jewelry store off Second Avenue in Billings in 2009. He threatened the middle-aged manager with a handgun, tossing a large pillowcase onto the glass counter. He was twenty-four at the time, a smart-ass, and wasn't going to leave the shop until he felt he had enough to make the next ten years of his life easier. It had been everything but easy, living on the street, after his parents lost their farm, a situation which sent his old man packing, whereabouts unknown, and his mother, into the arms of another man. Donald was too old to go chasing down his father, and too young to figure out how to save an abandoned potato farm. It didn't matter anyway, his father's whereabouts were unknown, and his mother's new relationship was cut short by her death, a sudden heart attack, so he did the one thing he knew he was good at, or at least thought he was good at – being a thief. He had been in and out of trouble since he was sixteen, first walking into a convenience store off Highway 212, where he ostentatiously strutted out with chips, candy, beer, and a pack of smokes. A year later, mugging a woman in a downtown alley, taking her purse with thirty-three dollars in it, and a third time, attacking a pizza delivery driver with a baseball bat, stealing two large pizzas, and seventeen dollars. Each time, he got caught. Authorities questioned why he thought robbing the local jewelry store would be any different. He was identified as the armed robber, and picked up within an hour, the collection of diamond rings and Rolex watches still in his possession. He pled guilty to a felony count of robbery with a firearm. Judge Molten sentenced Davis to six years in prison, instead of four years with two years of probation. He figured the extra time would do Donald some good; after all, he used to buy potatoes from his father, even went to high school with him. Now, the retired judge, knew Donald hadn't changed at all, and like his father, was nowhere to be found.

Aaron Bosman knew the games weren't over. He questioned why Donald, aka, Fajar ibn Wayne had dropped off the radar, fully aware of the fact that it had been nearly a month since the three Jehovah Witness Kingdom Hall bombings, but he couldn't close the case, not until Fajar was in custody for the bombings around Seattle, and not until the remaining forty-pounds of explosives had been

accounted for. The case would remain open. Indefinitely. Bosman

wasn't aware that wouldn't be much longer.

Chapter Twenty-Seven

This time, I felt reborn, a feeling that I was no longer inhabited by some other entity. I pushed the blinds open to the Spokane sky. Whatever was inside of me, had left, but I didn't feel alone.

I showered, pulled on a pair of spandex exercise capris, a lightweight t-shirt, a zip-up synthetic black jacket to block the April wind, and my new hiking shoes – Reeboks with gel bottoms. I drove to Division Street, parked my car, and boarded a white shuttle van with strangers. A day hiking around Hog Falls and the surrounding plateaus would do me some good. It was a five-mile hike up and down rocky paths, through treed areas that looked like they touched the clouds, and fields of wildflowers: bright yellow balsamroot, red-stems that dripped into tiny white Formosa flowers, and miniature white pentagram-shaped flowers that the group leader called shooting stars. I smiled, anxious to be with a group of people, and anxious to keep my body moving and in shape. I had been focusing more on myself lately, since learning my son had chosen to stay in Mogadishu, a decision he did without notifying family, and one I couldn't survive mentally unless I worked hard at it. The trip to Seattle, which had just ended, marked a new beginning for me, as I had finally come to the realization that the universe wasn't out to get anyone. *Sometimes things happen that people can't control.* I reminded myself, then quickly followed up with my favorite part. *But I can control my reaction.* I didn't know at the time, that I would be putting my new mantra to use right away. It wasn't until I had gotten home from the hiking trip, that I realized Mitch had sent an email, finally responding to one I had sent to his last known email. I took a deep breath, thinking about my day of balsamroot and tiny flowers that looked like they belonged in the sky, before opening my yahoo mailbox and reading. *I love you too Ma.* Nothing more. There weren't any answers to my questions: Are you still in Mogadishu? Are you safe? Is there a way to call you? None. There also weren't any responses to my statements: I was so worried about you. I'm glad the pirates didn't harm anyone. I'm sure it was scary. None. Five words were all I got; although, given the choice for any five words in the world I would take those. *I love you too Ma.*

He was isolating himself, and I wasn't chosen to be part of his circle, and neither was his sister. *I can control my reaction.* I thought as I played my new mantra over and over in my head. I exited my email, and shut down my computer, letting Mitch be alone, and letting my body absorb the fact that my adult son was gone.

#

Fajar had spent several weeks casing the one-story building off West Davison, had watched every employee come and go, knew their schedules, knew which programs were offered and on which days, and knew that Director Bosman seldom missed the adult program. Thursday Nights. Fajar had driven over 2,400 miles and would make every mile count. He had one goal – to make the thirteenth day of

April Bosman's last day. *Not even a blood transfusion will save him.*

He thought. *Not that he would accept one.*

#

I came face-to-face with Mount Hood the day after my hiking trip,

deciding I needed more open road, this one would be more than a

weekend trip, somewhere around a week. I had left my schedule

open. My gypsy lifestyle needed to be quenched, so I made my way

first to Oregon, wiggling around the massive mountain, its sharp

peaks hiding the stratovolcano's opening, a ticking bomb that could

erupt at any moment, sending a mixture of lava and ash into the

Clackamas River. Rolling hills surrounded me, highlighted in the

dark golds and virgin greens that showcased the first week of April. I

lost myself in a CD I had ordered off E-bay – *Everlast's Songs of the*

Ungrateful Living – while my head kept time with the raspy lyrics.

An earworm filled my head. *Heartbeats tick away* and *long and*

winding roads were still inside me, as I pulled over at the Taco Bell

in Redmond off 97 South. Biting into a hard-shell taco, I analyzed

the song: a cold reminder that life ends and our children continue

where we leave off. The thought made me miss them both more, but

I knew all I could do was be part of Allie's life and take care of myself. An invitation to see their new camping spot near Sacramento, California, included an eight-hundred-mile drive, but it was one I gladly accepted, especially after hearing about the arrival of Shiloh and Zeus' new puppies. I didn't stop driving until darkness surrounded me. By that point, exhaustion had set in, so I crawled in the backseat, under my normal array of blankets, and found sleep at the Herbert S. Miles Rest Area, tucked off Interstate 5, about two hours into California. My phone woke me when daylight first appeared.

"Mom, where are you?" The voice was almost twenty-two, not like the five-year-old I saw when my eyes were closed, the one full of sass and attitude.

"I'm just leaving Red Bluff, California," I announced, proud of the fact that I had made it around dangerous curves and dips, some which still showed signs of winter.

"Are you still willing to meet us in Sacramento?" She asked excitedly, revealing the fact that she was happy I had made it to the state where she and Reese had been working a new job, this one as a couple, taking care of a man's farm they had met in Oregon, guarding it in his absence, for over a month now, but were soon planning to head back to Oregon, within the next day or two, and wanted me to take the slow trip back with them, as we would sightsee along the coast. They were always on the move. *Who was I to judge?* I questioned. After all, I knew Allie had inherited my gypsy blood, the urge to roam and chase new beginnings.

"Absolutely," I answered. "I think I'm less than one hundred and fifty miles away." I couldn't wait to see her, to hug her almost twenty-two-year-old version.

"I love you Mom." She said. "I can't wait to see you." Allie continued. "The owner is coming back today, so we'll be camping on a piece of BLM land we know." She announced. "I'll text you the address."

"Okay, I'll see you at the address you send. Give me three or four hours." I paused long enough to remember what BLM stood for. *Bureau of Land Management.* I remembered discussing it with Allie, a good place to camp, free, without being asked to leave. "I love you too, Allie." Then I added. "Just stay there."

"Be careful, Mom."

"I will." I already knew, no matter how long my visit, that it was going to go way too fast. "I can't wait to see you and Reese." And then I remembered, "And, Shiloh and Zeus' new puppies."

Allie hung up the phone after telling me she loved me one more time. I kept my car pointed on 5 South, but I remembered it was important to take care of myself too, reaching Sacramento in just over two hours, but stopping at Pancake Circus off Broadway, where I devoured two biscuits with creamy white milk gravy, two large strips of bacon, and two over-easy eggs before arriving at the address Allie had texted me. When I pulled up, they were feeding ten hungry puppies. Allie looked beautiful, her wavy, dark hair, stretched down her back, and her skin, milky white, missed the summer sunshine, but glowed in the April breeze. Reese's hair had grown too, which he had meticulously formed in long dreads, some sporting wooden beads. The puppies fought for position, stampeding to the Chevy Tahoe's back open window, desiring my attention, but they had to wait. No one came before Allie. I wrapped my arms around her. My daughter.

#

Associate Deputy Director Aaron Bosman had been second in

command of the ATF office in Detroit for almost ten years. He

considered himself a police officer because he dealt with all the

same bullshit: sorting through evidence, investigating crime scenes,

testifying, and even participating in raids. Luckily, he had never

taken a life, something that was clearly against his religion. Carrying

a weapon made him cringe, and was only done out of necessity.

Taking someone's life, was something he knew he probably

wouldn't be able to do. He could tell some agents shied away from

him, wondering if he would have their back in a shoot-out. That's

why, most of the time, Associate Deputy Director Bosman was

confined to his office. Paperwork. Research. Fitting pieces together.

But lately, Bosman had been itching to locate Fajar, even if it meant

going out in the field himself. *Bloodguilt.* He reminded himself. *A*

crime in the eyes of God. He had listened to the elder preach last

night at the Jehovah Witness Kingdom Hall, taking it all in, still he

wanted Fajar to see prison once again, and if getting him there alive

would keep Bosman on the path to resurrection, something his faith

taught him was possible for the select few, then that was his ultimate

goal.

#

Enola watched the mixture of puppies – two solid white, five mostly black, one dark golden, one crème, and one black runt with white paws and a matching stripe down the center of its head – play in the golden field at Half Moon Bay, all the while watching the smiles on Allie and Reese. They looked happy with life, which was all Enola could ask for. Nothing else. The sun tickled the surrounding mountain tops, reminding them that evening was closing in, a fact that was reinforced by the way the sun glistened off the nearby lake, low and a bright yellowish-orange. It was time to make their way north on Coastal Highway 1.

It was nightfall before their caravan – a 2013 Hyundai followed by a 2002 Chevy Tahoe, pulling a 1970 style camper-trailer – pulled into San Francisco, where they stopped at a gas station to get water for Shiloh, Zeus, and the ten thirsty puppies, before making a quick run to Safeway, where Allie's saved Monopoly tickets were removed from her wallet and presented for a free box of Signature Pasta and a free loaf of Italian bread from the bakery, two of the ingredients for Reese's planned meal – Ground Beef and Sausage in spicy red sauce over angel hair pasta with a hunk of bread on the side. Reese and Allie paid for all the remaining food, a treat for Enola's first evening with them, one that would be spent at Vista Point in San Francisco.

Allie and Reese had become quite the survivalists, using their two-burner propane camp stove to cook a delicious meat sauce, one that tasted better than what is served in most Italian restaurants. They followed up dinner with a portable DVD family hour – *Dexter*, season seven, show number two – exactly where they had left off during Allie's last visit to Spokane. Enola felt comfortable hanging out with the two of them, there was no pretending; instead, her guard was down, and everything felt in sync, as a feeling of calmness filled Enola. They ended their evening with a walk around Vista Point, which provided a perfect view of the Golden Gate Bridge, before tucking puppies in their designated spot – a freshly cardboard-lined back section of their Chevy Tahoe, an area that served as a giant puppy pen. Enola retreated to the backseat of her Hyundai, hiding from the windy San Francisco forty-eight-degree temperature, after helping Allie walk Shiloh and Zeus, a chance to steal a few minutes alone with Allie.

Morning came early with tour buses, city buses, and tourists whipping their vehicles through Vista Point in San Francisco. Enola woke first in the back seat of her car, under three blankets, quickly sitting up to the crowded area. Listerine in hand, she opened the car door for a quick escape to the women's restroom. Cold windy air hit her face when she exited the vehicle, but she liked the way it made her feel – alive and alert. She combed her hair before returning to the back seat, where a new shirt was discreetly pulled on, a new match for the jeans she had worn for three days now. Allie and Reese stirred an hour later, feeding puppies, walking Shiloh and Zeus, and trying to make themselves presentable for a new day.

They caravanned up 101 North, weaving in and out of wine country, stopping at the Codding Town Center gas station for fuel and a couple of twenty-four-ounce I-cee drinks, before rounding the right side of Lake Sonoma, and cutting over to 128 West. By time they made Casper, California back on Coastal Highway 1, they were exhausted, but refused to settle for sleep in a mediocre parking lot. Instead, they drove another thirty minutes, before stopping at Taco Bell, and before stopping near Fort Bragg at a coastal access view. After another episode of *Dexter*, they car camped to the rhythm of crashing Pacific waves, and a view that couldn't be truly appreciated until morning.

Daylight displayed huge rocks that jutted toward the sky, crashing waves with tips that were iced with white foam, and steep mountain drop-offs that plunged down to the Pacific Ocean. The breathtaking site hugged their caravan, until roads merged, and they found themselves back on 101 North, again. They stopped at a Carl's Jr, ordering three super-stars with cheese, a vanilla milkshake for Reese, a strawberry milkshake for Enola, and an Oreo crème milkshake for Allie, enough to keep them going, until they were just north of Eureka, where giant redwood trees hid them from passersby. Enola enjoyed the freedom and simplicity, and she imagined eating macaroni and cheese and hotdogs prepared on a camp stove was ten times better than eating them in a modern kitchen, at least that's how she felt, as she devoured each bite. And, she knew that sleeping in a car, as cramped as it might appear, was more restful than sleeping in a hotel, as the sound of California rain played steadily on her Hyundai's roof. She fell asleep, unaware of the long-haul truckers that buzzed by in the wee hours of the night.

Routine is for people that have accepted slow death. Enola

wasn't one of them. Neither was Allie. Something was exciting

about getting up each morning without a plan, sometimes without a

direction, and never knowing how far the road would lead each day,

or what place and sounds would offer an adventurous night's sleep

each evening. They had spent four days together, four glorious days

of roads that dipped and weaved, a smorgasbord of sharp turns and

hidden treasures, roads that hung on the edge of the world, or so it

seemed, supporting *Hecataeus of Miletus'* theory – one where the

earth was flat. Enola's face glowed like a proud explorer, one that

had just discovered where nothingness began, until they entered the

south end of the Redwood National Forest, where ancient redwoods

changed her facial expression to one of reverence. Her Melantha

blues took in the gargantuan redwoods, their dark-skinned trunks,

stretching until the tips of each, mixed with the clouds. They pulled

their small caravan over, exiting vehicles long enough to capture

smiles in portraits, an arrangement of selfies, eyes glancing upward,

until a large Elk moved in the distance, redirecting the six eyes to a

field of Roosevelt elk, the females with dark brown heads, matching

the color of the redwood trunks that stood behind them. In a low whisper, Reese commented on the antlers, pointing out that some

seemed dipped in velvet. Enola put her arm around him, pulling him

closer, her silent hug thanked him for loving her daughter, and being

open to the magic wonders found in life. She wanted Allie to have

more, but as she looked out at the field of yellowish-brown rumps,

and redwoods that towered above them, she knew that was *more*.

Chapter Twenty-Eight

Roughly thirty-nine-and-a-half pounds of explosions were already in

place. Waiting. The Jehovah Witness Kingdom Hall, off West

Davison, was an older building. Fajar rented a solid white panel

truck, and a sixteen-foot ladder from a nearby Home Depot, items

that looked natural in the older Detroit neighborhood. The magnetic

sign he placed on the van, simply read: *Wayne's Construction*, added

humor, in his opinion, and a twenty-four-dollar expense that boosted

his disguise. It was Tuesday the eleventh, when Fajar climbed on the roof, in broad daylight, a large duffel bag fitted over his right shoulder, and a small toolbox was carried in the adjoining hand. Within minutes, he popped the head of the bowling ball shaped vent off its surface, exposing an abandoned bird-nest, which he quickly pulled out, and replaced with Asad's remaining forty-pounds of explosives, minus a half-pound stick of dynamite, the remaining piece, a leftover token, which represented the CSX explosives' heist. He rigged the explosives in place, making sure they didn't fall further down the large metal vent, and placed the large spinning silver top, that once covered it, in his near-empty duffel bag, now absent of all explosives, except for the eight-inch stick of dynamite. Before using the ladder to descend, Fajar made sure the vent stack was erect, especially after tampering with it, by securing a piece of pipe flashing around it. He had guessed the size, a three-inch adjustable piece, just the right fit to hold everything in place, probably not the best job, but he was sure it would hold the vent stack for another forty-eight hours.

#

Battery Point Lighthouse was the first thing I could see, as I sat up, after sleeping in the backseat of my car. The bright flash of white light, sent a blinding glare, a signal that even after years of mother nature's wrath – storms, waves, and even a 1964 tsunami – let the world know it was still standing, proudly, in Crescent City, the last major city on the northern California coastline before hitting Oregon. After puppy duty, and letting the dogs have some exercise, we made our way into downtown Crescent City, stopping at the information center, where we left my car, before making our way to Jedediah Smith Redwood's State Park in one vehicle.

The paved road became a mixture of dirt, sprawling tree roots, and loose rock once we were about eight miles from Stout Grove, accompanied by an occasional minefield of potholes, which hid around sharp corners and unexpected narrow roadway. I held on in the front passenger seat of Allie's Chevy Tahoe, as she maneuvered the steering wheel like a pro, while Reese, Shiloh, and Zeus bounced around in the middle bench section of the vehicle, and the sound of forty individual puppy paws could be heard sliding around on the morning's freshly laid cardboard in the open-trunk section. No animals were left behind for the day in their trailer, which Reese had detached and chained to the back of my Hyundai, parked across from the Chamber of Commerce. We operated under the *all or nothing* motto.

"I can't believe how big these redwoods are," I said excitedly, as we worked our way back into an area, that looked like part of the movie-set for *Jurassic Park.*

"It feels like we've entered a different dimension," Allie replied, before pulling her vehicle into a spot near hiking trails.

"The fur-babies want to explore," Reese announced before opening his passenger door, and letting Shiloh and Zeus bounce out into a scene from *Star Wars.* The other fur-babies, the ten that had finally found their footing, were issued a bowl of water and a large bowl of dried puppy kibble, before leaving down each window a good three inches, and before hurrying down a barely noticeable trail to locate Shiloh and Zeus.

"Shiloh is running like a greyhound dog." Allie laughed, watching her take corners at lightning speed in the distance, where Zeus tried to keep up. "Either that or a cheetah." She laughed again, referring to the way Shiloh would jump without hesitation over fallen trees and rocks the size of the Tahoe's tires.

"They're having a blast!" I exclaimed, as I smiled ear to ear and inhaled large gulps of redwood trees.

"I love you Mom." Allie reached for my hand, helping me down a steep part of the hidden trail, and past a redwood which was twice the length of my car.

"I love you too," I said. Then I stopped to face her, pulling her close, holding her tightly for as long as possible, before hearing the dogs off in the distance, and before thinking of a way to say what I wanted to say. "I want you to always be happy, and to always be safe." I looked into her Narducci brown eyes. "I love you Allie."

"I'm happy, Mom." She looked at me. "And, I love you too." She smiled a smile that melted my heart.

We spent several hours in Stout Grove, discovering several bright yellow banana slugs, tiny chipmunks, a brightly colored bluebird, a beetle that looked like it was dressed for a part in the movie *Beetle Juice,* and redwood trees that the three of us couldn't span across, even after extending our arms out to the sides, and touching fingertips to fingertips.

By the time we got back to the vehicle, the puppies had eaten every morsel of food and were sound asleep. Shiloh hopped in, exhausted, but made her way to the back of the Tahoe, where she laid down with her puppies, allowing each to suckle – ten puppies and ten nipples – the look on her face matched my thought. *They don't stay small forever.*

#

Director Bosman didn't have kids. Not yet. But, his wife Kathleen, was another four weeks away from giving birth to their first child. A son. Aaron Bosman, was excited, knowing that things would be different for his son, not like his childhood, where sports were off-limits. He wanted his son to be familiar with a game of basketball, maybe even an occasional game of softball, rather than spending his after-school hours placing *Watchtower* magazines on doors in surrounding neighborhoods. He believed in calling attention to God's kingdom, but he also believed children needed time to be children. That was something he never had, and something he wanted his son to experience. Kathleen Bosman agreed; although, she never disagreed with Aaron. She lived in his shadow, a silent figure in his life, spending her days preparing dinners and enough lunches to last her husband for the week at the busy ATF office. They never went out to eat, or anywhere for that matter, except on

Thursdays, when Kathleen would accompany Aaron to the Kingdom

Hall. Tonight, she was looking forward to hearing the lecture on

Armageddon by Elder Hansen. She was praying that his presentation

would fill her heart with hope, a verbal affirmation that the baby she

carried inside of her had a chance to be one of the 144,000 people

who would go to heaven, an exact number that devout JWs believed

would live with God. *Please God.* She was careful to keep her

thoughts to herself, but had been taught by her mother, that God

would only allow so many people into heaven after the imminent

end of the world. *Take my baby.* She thought.

#

Rain came down sporadically throughout the day, on their sixth day

of travel together, but it didn't matter. They had made their way to

North Bend, Oregon, after stopping at Harris Beach State Park to

play with the dogs, all twelve, and after stopping at Pistol River

South where they relaxed in a wooden fort, built on a tiny strip of

beach, by someone before them, probably to stay out of the cold

Pacific wind. They had stayed in the fort a few hours, playing with

Shiloh and Zeus, and two of the puppies that weren't sleeping, when

they left the vehicles in a nearby parking lot. Sand clung to the puppies' noses, as they made soft whimpers, which were drowned out by the sound of the Pacific. Enola let her face be licked, and her lap be crawled on, before exiting the fort, and brushing sand from the seat of her jeans. Moments later, and after dog bowls were refilled with water and kibble, they drove out the Rogue River Bridge and made their way to Cape Blanco. Allie wanted to climb up the spiraling stairs, to the top of Cape Blanco Lighthouse. Enola quickly agreed, but sensed Reese's hesitation, remembering that he was afraid of heights. Nevertheless, Reese agreed to make the climb to the top, where the three of them stood across from a park volunteer, an older gentleman, who seemed to have great respect for the landmark, and who explained where the lens got its name: Augustin Fresnel, the inventor. They listened, their bodies absorbing the heat, that reflected from the thick glass lens. Enola watched the light bounce off the giant lens as it turned, the bright rays of light hitting Allie's face, and showcasing her smile. *She looks happy.* Enola thought. *She's such a big part of my world.* She didn't know that the world was getting ready to end for some.

#

Mr. and Mrs. Bosman made their way inside the Jehovah Witness

Kingdom Hall. Fajar ibn Wayne had watched them both go inside, as

he sat in his white rental van, the magnetic sign facing Bosman's

parked vehicle, a new 2017 Nissan Sedan. The custom-made

magnetic sign didn't seem to cause a moment of concern, when

Bosman walked near, his only passing thought – *just another*

company logo: Wayne's Construction. Fajar waited, watching the

minute-hand on his father's cheap Timex watch, the only thing his

dad left behind, when he walked out on him and his mother. It was

6:55. He put the van in reverse, and slowly made his way around the

front of the building, past Bosman's Nissan, and near the back right,

away from the entrance, and away from possible witnesses. With his

driver's window down, he estimated the distance to the top of the

vent stack. *Somewhere around twenty-five feet.* He thought to

himself, an easy toss, for a man that had grown up on a potato farm.

Don't keep carrying that bucket son. He remembered his father

repeating. *Leave it at the end of each row, and toss 'em in.* He

pressed his foot down on the brake, keeping the van in drive, and for

a moment imagined a potato in hand, waiting. He lit the stick of

dynamic, holding it in front of his face, watching the flame work its way down the fuse, egging it on, before tossing it perfectly, and slowly driving away, toying with the fact that he knew the fuse was long enough for him to clear the parking lot. He rounded the back of the building, after watching the eight-inch stick drop inside the opened silver vent stack. Dead center. The first BOOM was loud, rocking the belly of the structure, as his van cleared the other side of the building, but he remained unscathed, his window still down, and was able to count several other explosions, as they sounded behind him. He didn't see anything in his rearview except flames, and a very distraught Aaron Bosman running back toward the building.

Chapter Twenty-Nine

The Umpqua River Lighthouse stood, facing the Winchester Bay. Its

silence stretched sixty-five-feet into the air, absent of people, and

behind a chain-link fence. Enola spotted the red lens, the color of fire

and bloodshed, a negative symbol exacerbated by the setting sun, but

only for a moment, until she looked away from it, and then back,

with a different point of view, her eyes seeing the structure's

strength, power, and passion for life.

Enola took Allie's free hand, as the three of them walked down a steep path toward Winchester Bay. The largest of the ten puppies was being cradled by Allie's opposite hand and arm, as it nestled near the left side of her chest, finding comfort in her heartbeat. Zeus and Shiloh ran ahead, trying to capture a large piece of driftwood that Reese was encouraging them to fetch.

"It's so beautiful out here Mom," Allie announced in a whisper, being careful not to wake the solid white puppy that had fallen asleep against her chest.

"Incredible." Enola squeezed the hand that she had been holding. "I love you so much," she said as she watched Reese tugging the nearly two-foot piece of driftwood from Zeus so that he could throw it again. This time in Shiloh's direction.

"I love you too." Allie squeezed back. "Thanks for spending time with me, Mom."

"I love spending time with you, Allie." She replied, noticing the sun had positioned itself directly over their heads, a signal that it was probably noon, plenty of time to make Road's End in Lincoln City.

There, Enola parked her Hyundai at one end of a four-mile stretch, then jumped in Allie's Tahoe, so she could park it at the other end, under two large shade trees. Inside were two adult dogs, ten yapping puppies, several bowls of water, and plenty of kibble. After positioning the windows down enough for adult dogs to stick their heads out, they started their four-mile walk.

The second Friday in April blew an ocean breeze at their faces, and white sea foam flirted with their six bare feet as they walked – feet that constantly stopped without warning, allowing the collection of tiny shells, pieces of abalone, several horned helmets, and five or six small conch shells. The four-mile stretch took them over two hours before they finally made it to Enola's car, where sandy feet welcomed rest, and sun-kissed bodies wanted a break from the coastal sun. After making their way back to the Tahoe, Enola watched Allie's routine: new puppy cardboard, more water, more kibble, and lots of kisses. She had performed the ritual several times a day for almost eight weeks. Soon, the puppies would be old enough to make it without their mother. *Like Mitch and Allie.* Enola thought. *No longer babies.* The proof was right in front of her.

#

Kathleen Bosman would never have the chance to raise her baby. Associate Deputy Director Aaron Bosman reached for the large brown paneled door, its round knob burned his skin, searing off several layers, and exposing bone. Still, he managed to enter the Jehovah Witness Kingdom Hall in Detroit. His first concern was to locate his pregnant wife, but within seconds, he crumbled to his knees, after his mind realized that the entire structure was gone, minus the singed door frame, which remained open behind him.

Firefighters, paramedics, police, and his entire ATF team were on site within fifteen minutes, but there was nothing left, except charred bodies and ash. Everything else was gone – his wife, his baby, Elder Hansen, and nineteen other members of his congregation. People he had grown up with. People he knew. People he loved. He was the only one who had survived. Pure luck. A quick trip to the car to put a box of Watchtower magazines in his trunk. His entire life taken. *Is this the beginning of Armageddon?* He questioned. His mind frantically searched for answers, while paramedics treated his hand, removing his wedding ring, and covering Bosman's hand in nonstick gauze.

"We have to transport you to the hospital sir." One of the paramedics instructed, as he helped him inside to a stretcher, and closed the door, leaving Bosman's team of field agents to search for the remains of his pregnant wife.

Bosman was numb to the severe physical pain he was enduring at the hospital, unaware that his left hand had been cleaned, and was now being meticulously scraped, as the surgical doctor on staff removed dead skin and tissue. His hand looked charred and leathery, but his awareness returned when he realized the nurse standing near him was preparing an IV.

"I won't be needing that." He said.

"Sir, it's just electrolytes to make your body keep functioning properly." The nurse in her twenties answered. "Just for overnight."

"I won't be staying overnight." He said, his mind suddenly fixated on the white van he had seen in the parking lot at the JW Kingdom Hall. His eyes widened as he remembered. *Wayne's Construction.* "Goddamn daddy's first name."

"I'm sorry sir." It was the third time she had been yelled at since dinner. Only two hours ago.

"That wasn't aimed at you Miss." He stood up, reaching for the phone near the hospital bed where he had been sitting, while the young nurse redressed his hand, after opening fresh nonstick gauze, another action he hadn't been unaware of. He dialed using his right hand, not his preferred hand, but the one that now showcased his wedding ring. Within minutes, his top field agent, Samuel Hopkins, was standing by his side and was escorting him from the hospital as instructed.

#

We reached Salem late that night and Portland less than an hour later, finding a rest stop off Interstate 5, where Allie admitted, with regret in her voice, that it was time to find the puppies good homes. She had helped Shiloh birth them, gently pulling out two of the ten, that were stuck in the birth canal, and giving mouth to mouth to one of the puppies that wasn't breathing when it entered the world. She had saved them out of love and out of kindness, and now, even though it was painful, she had to save them again. This time it would hurt more. Letting go was painful. I knew what she was going through. I knew the absence of losing something precious, small, and innocent. I was proud of her strength, as I watched her stand in front of a shopping plaza in Portland (a well-to-do area) with ten yapping

puppies. Her adult hands gave puppies to strangers, whose eyes

glistened for a chance to love something so little and virtuous. She

had fought with the hardest lesson in life – letting go. I put my arms

out to hold her as she and Reese made their way back to the spot in

the parking lot where I was parked near their Tahoe, the one that

held Shiloh and Zeus.

"It's okay," I said in her ear, her body crying uncontrollably

into mine. "You did the right thing," I reassured her, but all the while

knowing it didn't lessen the pain of losing something you love, an

unblemished soul, a piece of innocence.

"I should have kept a couple of them Mom." She cried into

my shoulder, already wet with her tears. "I should have." She

repeated.

"You just need to love on Shiloh now." It was an ironic

comparison that sent chills through my body. *Letting go of what*

needs to be elsewhere and loving what wants to be close. The

thought made a lump form in my throat, as I pictured their lives

progressing – their innocence stripped away, their bodies weathered

by time and hardships, and their trust for others hidden behind growls and aggressive behavior. "She needs you," I said loudly,

somewhat for myself, as I thought about how Allie and Mitch were

like grown puppies, how all adults are. Innocence gone. Bodies

weathered. And trust hidden behind our aggressive lifestyles. I held

her tighter, just to let her know I would always love her.

#

The next morning Enola woke around nine, before Allie or Reese,

her body enjoying the early morning silence, and hoping that Allie

wasn't still suffering from adult decisions. She wanted the last day of

her visit with them to be special, a day the three of them had agreed

would be well spent at Multnomah Falls, a hidden gem in Oregon.

The waterfall could be seen from the interstate, but only a glimpse of

it; the remainder was reserved for people that were willing to

complete the hike, just over a mile, straight up.

They got to the parking lot around noon, located leashes for

Shiloh and Zeus in the pull behind trailer, and made their way

through the man-made tunnel to the south side of the interstate, to

the beginning of what would turn out to be a very narrow, very

challenging, and very steep incline to the top of the waterfall. At

first, it didn't look like the walk could be that challenging, just

standing at the base of the over 600-foot waterfall, one that roared
like a lion and spit water like a whale, but it held secrets in the
winding path that carved its way up the mountain.

Benson bridge – a small bridge named after a man who
owned the waterfall during the early 1900s, was their first stopping
point, only a few hundred feet into their journey. Cold mist sprayed
their faces and dampened Shiloh's black three-inch fur and slid off
Zeus' shortened black and white coat. The roar was louder and more
powerful than witnessed from ground level, and yet their walk had
just begun, one that would become much more challenging, and one
that would require time-out breaks on large rocks and downed trees
just to catch the breath that altitude had sucked out. By the time they
reached the top of Multnomah Falls, over two hours had passed.
Enola stood at the edge of the platform at the top, looking down at
the powerful display of water, as it made its way to a new beginning.
She thought about a sign she had read near the bottom of the falls,
one that explained why the falls were created, according to the native
Americans. *That would do it for me.* She thought, smiling to herself,
as she remembered reading about why the falls were created – *to win
the affection of a young Indian princess who wanted a private place*

to bathe. Enola smiled at the thought. *He'd have my heart.* She chuckled, before snapping several photos of the falls: one as it plunged 600 feet toward the ground, one of Allie and Reese, one of Shiloh and Zeus, and, with the help of Reese's long arm, a selfie of the three of them.

#

His agents were all over the white van, had tracked it to the rental company, had tracked the ladder to Home Depot, and even had Fajar ibn Wayne on camera buying a three-inch adjustable piece of pipe flashing. The van had been impounded for evidence. And, one of the agents had just called to let Bosman know he had a copy of the order form for the magnetic sign. It was a done deal. He would get life in prison, many times over, which Bosman was too choked up to comment on one way or another, but the other agents knew this would be one case where Aaron Bosman wouldn't be happy about Michigan not having the death penalty. *The fucker killed my wife and baby.* Bosman kept his thoughts to himself, as he tried to stay focused on finding him. An APB was out, and a gas station employee had called the local PD, after eyeing an unzipped duffel bag, lying in the back seat of a brown Chevy, with a large metal vent cover propped in the middle, something he wouldn't have given two

shits about, except that the man had seen his eyes, and was furious.

"What the fuck are you staring at?" Fajar grilled the gas

station employee.

"Nothing sir. Just noticed you have one of those roof turbine

vents." The unshaven gas attendant quickly answered. "My brother-

in-law owns the company that makes those."

"Who fucking cares." He threw a twenty at the man, before

driving away, leaving the attendant standing there, shaking his head

at the Montana plates. Fifteen minutes later, he was on the phone to

his brother-in-law, talking shit about the rude asshole from Montana,

the same brother-in-law that had just given one of Bosman's agents

information about the Jehovah Witness Kingdom Hall's ventilation

system. Sometimes the universe helps track bad guys. Five minutes

after that, the owner of Turbine Vents was back on the phone with

the agent. And within seconds, Associate Deputy Director Bosman,

who was ignoring Deputy Director Innisbrook's repeated

instructions to *sit this one out*, and several undercover cars, were

heading east on Interstate 94. They couldn't be more than thirty-

minutes behind him.

Chapter Thirty

Aafa Idris, whose first name meant forgiving, had just finished

evening prayers with her husband and two small sons, in the small

village of Moman, before sitting down to a meal of Samoosi Yirakot,

a recipe she had perfected, one that was passed down from her

mother, turnovers stuffed with diced potatoes, onion, cauliflower,

carrot, peas, and green beans, a treat her family always looked

forward to on Thursday nights following prayer. She had been in bed

with her husband, almost five hours, by the time the MOAB hit the eastern region of Afghanistan, 4 a.m. (UTC), Coordinated Universal Time. It was nine hours earlier in Detroit, around the same time that Associate Deputy Director Aaron Bosman watched the Jehovah Witness Kingdom Hall go up in flames, his wife and unborn son inside, as well as nineteen other members of the congregation, and Elder Hansen, who had just started speaking about Armageddon. Unbeknownst to Bosman, Armageddon was not only occurring in front of him but also seven thousand miles away, across the Atlantic, a decision made by the new POTUS, Donald Trump, an ordered strike on ISIS. There was no warning for Aafa or her family. She didn't die instantly, like the rest of her family; she lived seconds more, enough time to see Allah's face while her heart was still beating. She smiled knowing her punishment would be brief, knowing that Allah spares those who die on Thursday night, and into Friday, holding all punishment for Judgment Day. For that, she was grateful.

#

It took three days to catch up with Fajar ibn Wayne. He was a cocky son-of-a-bitch, moving at a much slower pace than what agents had anticipated, and had switched to Interstate 80, a move that was noticed by an undercover patrolling that route. It was a good save, but something Bosman expected, as he knew there were only so many routes, and there were a lot more UCs out there. *Let me make this clear.* Bosman said into the phone. *Wait until I fucking get there.*

They did. Two locals from the Joliet Police Department, Detroit Agent Hopkins that had called him after being notified by the UC, and another undercover from Detroit Metro. The four had been staking out Fajar's room, avoiding media, and avoiding attention. *Lie low.* Bosman's orders. *Wait.*

Associate Deputy Director Aaron Bosman pulled up sooner than expected, having used a single blue light on his vehicle to break all speed limits, even though against policy, but he didn't care. He pulled into the Motel 6 parking lot off McDonough Street, his light no longer visual, his approach quiet, his left-hand throbbing, as he refused all pain medication, and his jaw clenched, mostly anger. It was a 2-star motel, which Aaron thought was above Fajar's social class. He watched the glow from the television play peek-a-boo with the one-inch gap underneath the cheap rubber-back curtains, not enough to see anyone in the room, but just enough to suspect someone was in there. Agent Samuel Hopkins knew emotions were running high, he also knew his boss wasn't carrying a gun, something they had talked about in the hospital, and something Aaron Bosman adamantly refused to do, not in this situation. *It would be too tempting.* He had made the statement several times, and only in the presence of Agent Hopkins, a man he considered a personal friend, someone he knew had his back and someone who was now crouched beside him in the dark.

"I'll approach alone," Bosman whispered. "You cover me."

"That's a polite fuck you, Sir." The agent didn't take his eyes off the motel door as he answered back to his boss. "I know you're not carrying." He whispered, making sure the local police and UC from Detroit Metro weren't privy to the information. "You'd be a sitting duck."

"I'm the only one he'll let close," Bosman announced. "Bloodguilt." Aaron had known Agent Hopkins for years, had shared the JW belief about bloodguilt. "He knows he's safe with me." Aaron sounded convincing. "I can bring him in alive." Then he played his best card. "Kathleen would want that."

The night sky had settled at ten p.m. by the time Aaron

Bosman approached room 144. He didn't knock. Instead, he used his

deepest voice, one he knew Fajar would recognize.

"Donald Jay Davis." He wasn't going to give him the

satisfaction of using his Muslim name. "It's Director Bosman." He

paused. Listening for movement. "You were right about the

keychain." He spoke loudly to the door that was still closed, as he

stood shielded behind a square column, only four feet from the door,

as he peered around the sharp pieces of stucco, that up-close looked

like white frosting, his wife's favorite. "You're a smart man." It

killed Aaron Bosman to say that. "You know I'm the only one out

here unarmed." He watched the glow from the television disappear.

"You are surrounded." He hoped the four badges that crouched in

the parking lot fit the definition of being surrounded. "I'm your only

chance out of here alive." He felt his jaw clenching again. "My

pregnant wife would want that." The door opened, just enough for

Bosman to stick his gauzed hand inside. "I'm coming in."

"Shut the fucking door." Fajar wanted a moment with

Bosman. "Don't come any closer." He was calling out orders. "And,

don't turn on any fucking lights." Aaron glanced at him. Standing in utter darkness, except for a dimly lit bathroom, which stood unoccupied. They were alone. "I meant to kill you," Fajar announced.

"I know." He studied the hatred in Donald's face.

"I hate your type." He said, his nose twitched, something Aaron could see even in the poorly lit beam of light that stretched from the bathroom.

"What type is that?" Aaron Bosman wanted an answer.

"You're too afraid of your God." He smirked. "You make me sick." He looked at Bosman with disgust. His tone was hateful, and his eyes grew angry. That's when the sound of three-gun shots filled the air. POW. POW. POW.

Within minutes, the four badges that had been waiting, guns drawn, invaded room 144.

#

By May, Enola pined to see Hope, British Columbia, Canada, a destination she had passed on her way home from Edmonton, two months back, when she found out life had changed for Dixie, and when she had last shouted at the sky in anger. *Stage four melanoma.* She remembered Dixie's announcement. *It has spread to several lymph nodes.* Now, after further phone conversations with Dixie, she needed to surround herself in a town that she felt might bring some peace.

She was in her new Jeep Cherokee Sport by four a.m., also red, but much better at handling Washington's landscape, heading to the spot where she knew the roads diverged, the exact location that had taunted her with a small sign, one word, *HOPE*, with an arrow, pointing northwest; so now, retracing her tracks, she exited Washington state, and made her way back past the Coulee Dam, only this time, the backdrop was a sunrise, instead of a sunset. Again, she pulled over, watching as the morning rays reflected deep into the surface of the water below, allowing it to become part of her. She smiled before calling Allie.

"Hey darling," Enola said to her still twenty-two-year-old daughter. "I wanted to let you know I'm headed into Canada for a few days."

"Good for you Mom," Allie replied. "You deserve it." She knew about Hope, Canada, knew the story of how her mother had spotted the sign, and knew her mother fought with faith, a fight that Allie had participated in many times herself. And, she knew, just from knowing her mother, that Hope, Canada would eventually be crossed off her mother's to-do list.

"Thanks Allie." She paused. "I'm not sure how my cell phone reception will be, so I thought I'd give you the heads up." She still had MetroPCS, and still paid extra to have the plan where she could use some of the phone towers in Canada, so at least there was a chance, a chance to keep in contact with the world she was leaving behind for a few days.

"Okay Mom." Allie sounded like she was having a good day. "Just drive carefully and know I love you."

"I will." And then, "I love you too Allie."

Enola drove her two-week-old vehicle, a purchase she had recently made, something better for the Spokane winters, to 155 North, then 97 North, before hitting Tonasket where mountains welcomed her. By noon, Enola reached Hope, Canada, first stopping at Slide Mountain, where she studied the rawness of mother nature, a mountain stripped of its trees, its soul exposed, nothing but rock, a scene that at first glance looked like it might make an adrenaline junkie's favorite slide, but a scene that corrected itself after Enola read the plaque at the foot of the mountain. *Earthquake. 1965.*

Mudslide. Debris. And the part that Enola replayed in her mind one more time before getting back in her Jeep Cherokee – *Four dead.* A reminder not to take life for granted.

Her second stop – the Othello Tunnels, created in 1915, a series of three, each in its own mountain of solid rock – piqued her curiosity, enough to stop, and enough to walk the trail back to the tunnels. The first one she entered, reminded her of Dacey Fears – dark, cold, unforgiving, with a surface where her Reeboks fought with uneven rock, slightly causing her left ankle to twist, causing extra strain on her left knee, as the visual of his angry face stood near her, his right arm administering force, his hand holding a wooden bat, an instrument that would be used to teach her a lesson. *Sexual exploration is evil.* She recalled the pain and confusion in the darkness but kept walking toward the light, unfazed, her only focus on the beauty that awaited her – tall trees that blew in the wind, and water that kicked up in the fast-moving Coquihalla Canyon River. Then she entered the second tunnel, where once again, her mind played games on her, the energy in the tunnel was all-consuming, with hidden spots, absent of light, the unknown surrounded her, the sound of dripping water could be heard in the damp corners, the smell of acetone entered her nasal passages, its odor like the smell of

death. She thought of her mother – Melantha. *She used a piece of the*

broken saucer that Nurse Halohand had left behind. She wiped a

tear from her eye, remembering Doctor Stevens' declaration about

her mother's suicide. *We're sorry for your loss.*

Enola stood on the second bridge that connected with the

final tunnel for almost twenty minutes, a chance to compose herself,

as she watched a bird soar overhead, until it landed in a tall pine, and

as she listened to the powerful roar in each turn of the Coquihalla

Canyon River. She waited until nature took the bad memories away

and replaced them with peace. Then she entered the final tunnel. It

was the shortest one. Its walls looked strong, fearless, and it

welcomed Enola with the light that shined through from the opposite

end. She walked inside at a slower pace, absorbing its strength, and

touching the interior walls – warm, inviting, rich in character,

reminding her of Grover Starks, her biological father.

She breathed in a big gulp of air upon exiting, as she

wandered down a nearby trail, searching for the perfect tree along

the Coquihalla Canyon River, one she knew Dixie would like. She

pulled out a pocket knife, that she had been carrying, and proceeded to carve into the massive tree, its trunk at least seven foot in diameter. She worked the blade of her knife into the tree's outer skin. **DLD.** She stood back, making sure it was perfect. *Dixie Louise Durant.* She took a few minutes admiring her work, rubbing her hand on the newly tattooed spot. *Now, Dix will always be a part of Hope.* She thought. *Maybe the stage four melanoma will see this and leave her alone.* She said the last words out loud, hoping nature would hear her, then shut her eyes, asking for her biological dad's help, remembering how good he was at persuading people to do what he wanted. *Use your attorney know-how.* She thought as she watched the river explode, forming small white caps.

She left feeling satisfied that either nature, hope, or Grover would take care of Dixie. By four in the afternoon, she was walking on foot, down Wallace Street in the town of Hope, looking in gift stores, snapping photos of all the life-size wood carvings, (her favorite was the one with an eagle, wolf, and a bear) which lined Wallace, and making her way to food – The Golden Star for Chinese. By nightfall, she was in lying in the back of her Jeep Cherokee Sport, the middle seats folded flat, giving her extra room, as she stared at the crescent moon, perfectly placed over a snow-capped mountain, a typical site, even in early May, in the center of

Squamish, Canada. And by morning, she was pulling a third blanket

up to her neck, absorbing warmth, an attempt to avoid feeling the

chilly temperature. She made her way to a gas station, within view,

where she recharged: first, a much-needed bathroom break, then a

sixteen-ounce cup of light hazelnut coffee, topped with a fresh

cranberry-lemon muffin. Now, she had the strength to continue – 99

West to Whistler.

Chapter Thirty-One

Samuel Hopkins walked into Bosman's office. This time it wasn't to see his best friend and boss. This time it was to give a final answer to the question he had repeatedly been asked by Deputy Director Innisbrook, a half-dozen times over the course of the last month, and was now being asked a seventh time. This time in person.

"Do you want the wallpaper changed out?" Innisbrook paused. "A different desk?"

"No." He shook his head. "I'm content with Bosman's office exactly as is."

"It's your office now, Associate Deputy Director Hopkins." He was delicate, but assertive, reminding Samuel Hopkins that he had taken Aaron Bosman's place, as the Associate Deputy Director of the Detroit office. Now he called the shots under Innisbrook.

"I know Sir, it's just hard to wrap my head around Bosman."

"It was time," Innisbrook said the words with certainty, leaving no room for doubt, before leaving the new associate deputy director sitting in the leather executive chair, now *his*.

Samuel sat there, his eyes drawn to the left-hand corner of his desk, where the Fajar ibn Wayne file now rested. He had reviewed the facts at least a thousand times in his head. He knew. Knew that Aaron Bosman, his friend, had shot Fajar ibn Wayne three times, once in the left shoulder, once in the chest, and a third time in the right temple. He also knew that Bosman's right hand had been swabbed for gun residue. Positive. The bureau said he was lucky, making three quick shots, with his non-dominant hand, after having to forcefully wrestle the thirty-one-year-old ex-potato farmer and ex-con for the gun, again with one good hand. Pure luck. *Bullshit.*

Agent Hopkins knew better. He had spent the last two years earning a criminal law degree at Harvard, while serving as an agent with ATF, and had sat in on some of the best research studies performed. **The dominant hand is ALWAYS used in zero-reaction-time situations, regardless of pain or previous injuries.** It was something his favorite law professor said repeatedly. He knew Bosman had carried the .380 ACP into the room, knew he had probably been the one to file off the serial number, and knew he had shot Fajar three times, consecutively, without batting an eye, and with prior knowledge that he was going to do so, before entering the motel room. Premediated. What he didn't know were two things. One – how to prove it. And, two, whether he even wanted to. Aaron Bosman had stepped down from his position, after being asked to by Deputy Director Innisbrook, unhappy that he was in the room alone with Fajar, and beyond pissed off that he was even involved with the case, after being told repeatedly to stay out of it. Last he heard, Bosman was in California, where, he wasn't sure; although, he knew Human Resources had forwarded his personal items from his office and other paperwork.

#

Whistler, Canada was a last-minute addition to my travels. A destination, the locals of Hope informed me, would have more inuksuk statues, like the one I had seen near Wallace Street. I had first noticed the tiny human-shaped landmark, as I walked across the street, its man-made design inspired my thoughts, a symbol, which clearly showed how things fit together, a balancing act, and as I learned from one local gift-shop owner, a historic marker, one that signaled direction for lost and hungry travelers. Still, I imagined there was a deeper meaning, one I wanted to explore, so I made my way to Whistler, another three hours northwest.

Curves and dips nipped at my Cherokee's tires, rings of thick white puffy clouds flirted with the tops of the mountains out my left driver's window, and May snow still painted the tallest peaks. I made it to Vancouver by noon, where I stopped, pulling over to the side of the road, slowly down a steep embankment that overlooked the water around Vancouver's tallest skyscrapers. It looked like a city a person could easily get lost in, so I only admired it from a distance, keeping my sites on Whistler. Ninety more minutes.

#

Aaron Bosman had rented a studio with one bath, off Russia

Avenue, in San Francisco, for thirteen hundred a month, half of his

monthly pension, but he didn't care. It was temporary, another ten

months on the lease, time enough to figure out where he should go,

without his wife, without his baby, and without his faith. *I've lost*

everything. He thought. It had been a major decision to leave

Michigan and move 2,400 miles, but he needed to be in California,

for reasons he wasn't willing to talk about, and he needed to be away

from Michigan. First, he knew too many people there. Second, he

didn't want to walk into the new Jehovah Witness Kingdom Hall on

West Davison, the one he had heard was almost finished being built.

It was a much smaller building, but would still feel empty,

accommodating nineteen less members, twenty-one including

Kathleen Bosman and his unborn son, and twenty-two if he counted

himself. The new JW Kingdom Hall would be sufficient for the

survivors, those that hadn't attended the April thirteenth massacre.

Elder Tanner, the new head elder, appointed by the

remaining congregation, sent the ATF office a large manila

envelope. Inside, were four things: a photo of the new building, a

thank-you note for the bomb squad's hard work, a photo of a large fountain and plaque built at the exact spot where human remains had been removed, and a private letter sealed and addressed to Aaron Bosman. Now, Bosman was sitting in his studio apartment in San Francisco, opening the letter, dated a few days earlier, which had been forwarded from ATF's personnel office. It read:

May 10, 2017

Dear Mr. Bosman:

*This letter is to inform you that you are no longer considered a member of The Jehovah Witness Kingdom Hall. This decision was made by the Board of Elders (BOE). You may not attend services, study groups, or **any** functions related to **any** JW organization. I am sure you understand the seriousness of committing bloodguilt; it is not something that can be tolerated, under any circumstances. Your failure to remain loyal to your faith has caused irreparable damage to your soul.*

Regretfully,

BOE & JW Associates

Aaron glared at the letter. He knew he had taken a life. It was intentional. *The mother-fucker deserved to die.* He thought. *I'm glad I did it.* And then, *he never expected I'd have a gun.* Aaron should feel shame, knowing that his life of faith had ended, but he felt relief, welcoming Armageddon, the imminent end, inevitable according to the JW faith. He reclined his living room chair, extended his legs on the footrest, crumpled the letter into a loosely formed ball, and tossed it in the trash, before grabbing the small black remote, and searching for news, anything to distract his thoughts. *Why am I really in California?* He questioned, although he knew the answer. He stared at Donald Trump's face, as he listened to reporters grill him. *Do you think dropping the MOAB bomb on the eastern region of Afghanistan was a good decision?* He watched Trump circle around an answer. *How many innocent civilizations were killed?* He turned off the television before a response was given. It was decided. *Armageddon.* It didn't matter anymore.

#

In the center of Whistler, at Florence Petersen Park, stood a bright green sign with a large pink-winged dragonfly, which captured Enola's attention. Bright yellow buttercups, early blue violets, and rich orange poppies lined the park's walkway. It was a relaxing stroll, leading out to a giant inuksuk statue, where Enola snapped a photo, capturing the morning sun, as it reflected off the *Iron Man* look-a-like's head, sending two solid rays of sunlight down the center of his body. It looked powerful.

By eleven a.m., Enola was on an open-air chairlift, headed up Blackcomb Mountain. The Wizard Express carried her high above the snow-covered peaks and deep ridges, over the heads of skiers, and up to the very top of Blackcomb, a procedure that was completed after boarding the Seventh Heaven Shuttle Bus, which worked her as close to the peak as possible. Another inuksuk, stood in the distance, its backdrop an endless valley of snow-covered peaks, dips, and volcanic landscapes. *Beautiful.* She thought. Standing seven thousand feet above the world below, Enola studied the figure, this one made of six large boulders, and towering almost three times her height. The legs of the inuksuk were long boulders selected for their rectangle shape. Its lower abdomen was a replica, except the placement was horizontal, instead of vertical like the legs. A smaller boulder was used for the stomach, but Enola knew looks were deceiving, and could tell that even one boulder couldn't be lifted by the strongest man she knew. It was too heavy. And, the large slab of rock that balanced above it, was selected for its shape, and extended past the width of each leg, giving the figure a look of having extended and welcoming arms. The sixth boulder was centered directly at the top, and represented the figure's head. For Enola, it was a symbol of nature and humanity; it was a symbol of hope.

Enola caught the peak-to-peak gondola lift from Blackcomb Mountain to Whistler Mountain. It was only a fifteen-minute ride, and swayed over a mixture of patches, a very confused month of May, some snow and some green grass, where Enola spotted two black bears frolicking, her first time to see bear in the wild, since she was a kid, and since leaving the mountains of Asheville, North Carolina behind her.

The gondola dropped her off within visual distance of another inuksuk, this one composed of five boulders: two long rectangular legs, one rectangular boulder that served as a stomach, one longer boulder that represented its outreached arms, and the fifth, a chunky boulder for the head. She imagined it wasn't the number of boulders that was important; it was the fit, one relying on the other. The realization came to her, as she stood in the location known as the Top of the World Summit. She breathed in massive amounts of high-altitude, before making her way on foot, down a steep forty-minute trail, where she boarded another gondola, this one

to a small restaurant, where she downed a hot bowl of goulash.

Enola let the warmth of the beef and potato goulash melt her inside

chill, before rinsing it down with a bottle of coke, an opposite effect,

and then wandered into a small jewelry shop where she made a

purchase – a silver chain and pendant. The pendant, a small, flat,

replica, of an inuksuk statue, caught her eye, its body made of

sterling silver boulders, a symbol of hope for humanity, and

something she proudly wore around her neck.

#

I arrived home a few days later, my doormat littered with a Sunday

paper, a few days old. I carried it into my small studio apartment,

settling on my daybed, where I stretched out with an unsweet tea,

and the urge to thumb through the nationwide section, a way to

unwind after driving since early morning, and a way to see what

major news stories I had been missing. I noticed the article right

away: **Missing Explosives Case Closed – Associate Deputy**

Director Aaron Bosman steps down. I read. Read about the stolen

explosives off the CSX train, read about the numerous bombings

which had involved some of the explosives, including the recent JW

Hall bombing in Detroit, read about how the suicide bomber in New York was the one who masterminded the heist, and read about how authorities suspect he shot and killed his brother as he exited a Detroit mosque. That's when I turned the page, flipping to 1-C, where four small photos were tagged at the end of the article. One of former Associate Deputy Director Aaron Bosman, one of Fajar ibn Wayne, one of Asad Harb, and one of Bobby Harb, *my Bobby*, a purple dandelion.

Chapter Thirty-Two

Eleven Weeks Later

The sixth of August sky in Spokane was hazy, causing Enola's blue

eyes to itch, eyes that had turned fifty-six. Allie had called early to

wish her mother a happy birthday. Enola had thought about making

her way to Oregon, where Allie and Reese were working and being

parents to Shiloh and Zeus, but she felt surrounded by the fires that

were burning above her in British Columbia, to the east of her in

Western Montana, and to the southwest of her in Yakima,

Washington. She felt fenced-in. The mountains across from her

balcony were hidden by the smoky visitor, and the air was too thick

and heavy to breathe, prompting her to close the glass sliding door

she usually left open. There was a part of her that wanted to escape,

a feeling she had felt many times before, but she knew her options

were limited. She couldn't go north. She couldn't go south. She

couldn't go east. Many roads were closed due to visibility. Her only

option, she calculated, was due west, but even that direction would

be like going from bad to worse, as Seattle had been making the

news all week. *Extreme health risks.* She remembered. *Seattle is*

sitting under smoke. Her thoughts left the smoke-filled sky and

traveled over 8000 miles away, searching for Mitch, wishing he

would call, fearing for his safety, and longing for a relationship with

a son she felt she had lost.

#

Two weeks later, I was on my way to Allie, first to celebrate my

recent birthday, and second, to see the Great American Eclipse. I got

to Aurora, Oregon late on the eighteenth, a Friday, while Allie and

Reese were taking an after-work shower at the TA Travel Center,

something they routinely did. I pulled into the parking lot, before locating their Tahoe and camper, and then parked nearby, so I'd see them when they came out. I reclined my driver's seat, leaning back, and thinking I would shut my eyes, but only long enough to catch a twenty-minute power nap. I was wrong. I woke to Allie's tap on my window, an hour later. I smiled as I up-righted my seat, and quickly exited my still new vehicle, giving her a long-overdue hug, her hair wet, smelling of coconut shampoo. Reese reciprocated, by offering a hug of his own, after checking out my new vehicle, his smile noting his approval. Both of them agreed the Cherokee suited me better, as a Washington resident.

I followed them to their usual camping spot, about five minutes down the road, a parking lot surrounded by trees, that welcomed overnight camping. Free. A good deal for two young working adults, trying to figure out how to survive in today's economy, which we all agreed, was one step at a time. It didn't take long, after pulling into our claimed spots, before Shiloh and Zeus recognized my voice, and fought to leave the confines of their napping area, their tails and long tongues anxious to see me. I obliged.

We settled into comfortable sitting positions inside their camper, as the time approached midnight, yet none of us had eaten since lunch. I was happily surprised, as Reese opened a large bag, revealing a Popeye's chicken box, with an assortment of spicy and regular chicken inside, a large container of mashed potatoes, and three biscuits, all perks from knowing the right people within the TA Travel Center. I watched Allie open their large blue and white cooler, exposing an assortment of canned soda and bottled water. I graciously pulled a bottle of water free from the ice. We were all set, taking up where we had left off months before, unguarded familiarity, and unmonitored conversation, apparent from the steady flow and laughter, which filled the small camper, until almost two a.m. It was easy to spend time with them, even when the rest of the world seemed to be sleeping.

"Goodnight mom." Allie gave me one last hug, before I excited their camper, and made my way to the open space in the back of my Jeep Cherokee. "Tomorrow we will celebrate your birthday." An announcement I followed with a smile.

"Okay, sweetie," I said, knowing Allie never did anything half-ass. I knew she had a plan.

By ten a.m. I knew I was right. My instructions were explicit.
"There are restrooms over there." Allie pointed. "We'll be leaving in
about an hour." She informed me. "I have to feed Shiloh and Zeus,
and let them potty." She kept the dogs on a routine.

"Do I get to know where we're going?" I asked.

"Absolutely not," she replied quickly. "It's a surprise."

An hour later, I was following them, but only for twelve
miles, before parking in a large field, the camper pulled directly
under a shade tree, where Shiloh and Zeus were left with water,
food, and open camper windows, inviting the cross breeze to stop on
its way through. I spotted fields of endless color across the street,
and a sign, which as we got closer, I could read: The Dahlia Festival
2017. I glowed. Allie knew me. Knew the kinds of things that made
me smile. Forty acres of dahlias did the trick. Reese and Allie paid
for three tickets, and I followed them, into a large building, just after
the admission booth, where dahlias of every color and size were
arranged in visual presentations. Each display was labeled with the
name of the dahlia. I had never seen so many different types: crème
tips popped from cups of sunset-red, off-white tips sprung from
dark-blood-red, bright yellow stood center stage in velvet orange,

hot pink melted to a painter's palette of dark green, four shades of red exploded from one, soft snowy white dripped from another, and a mixture of violet and tan commanded attention. My favorite, a dark burgundy with a bright yellow center, glistened; its center appeared to be sprinkled with pixie dust, giving it a magical appearance. I read its name – *The Tahoma Moonshot.*

"They are amazing Allie," I said.

"I never expected to see so many colors Mom." She commented.

We remained in the building for over an hour, joking about *The Redd Devil*, admiring *The Vixen* displayed by a large plastic Santa, commenting on *The Hot Rod*, and craving something to drink after coming across *The Ice Tea*, a large peach-colored dahlia, before heading outside to the forty-acre field. I watched the sun reach down from the Oregon sky, greeting each flower, mimicking the bees, as the golden-bodied insects, with black stripes neatly placed around their abdomens, floated from flower to flower. There were also bumble-bees, their wings neatly tucked behind jet-black middles, with legs that hooked together, like little chia seeds. *Connections.* I thought once again. *Everything is connected.*

#

Aaron Bosman had discarded the letter from the JW Hall. He had

dismissed his faith. *Donald Jay Davis, was wrong about me.* He

thought. *I don't fear my God.* He picked up his car keys, absent of

the round metal disc with the universal emblem denoting NO blood.

He had tossed it in the same small trash can, another sacred promise

broken, now it joined the crumpled JW letter, and one other item –

the legal document that he had carried in his wallet, for decades, to

inform hospitals and doctors that he couldn't accept a blood

transfusion. Everything had been discarded. His wife. His baby. His

career. His faith. He reached for the small revolver laying on his

nightstand. This time it was a .38 special, and this time he wouldn't

bother filing off the serial number. He was less than six hours from

his destination, his reason for moving to California.

#

We lined our vehicles up outside the locked gate, the entrance to The

Willamette Mission State Park in Gervais, by six a.m. on Monday, a

location that was in the path of totality, to see The Great American

Eclipse. It was the twenty-first of August, 2017. The Oregon park

officials waived the five-dollar fee per car, motioning us through:

vehicle number seven, a bright-red 2017 Jeep Cherokee Sport – and

– vehicle number eight, a slightly-faded blue 2002 Chevy Tahoe

pulling a small camper. I could see the heads of Shiloh and Zeus

hanging out the Tahoe's passenger windows in my rearview. Shiloh

directly behind Allie's driver's seat, and Zeus preferred the window

behind Reese. Allie kept close pace to my back bumper. There were

another four or five hundred vehicles behind us, being corralled into

a straight line, by park staff, waving LED traffic control wands. By

eight in the morning, there were another two or three hundred

vehicles in the field marked day-use only. Tents were in the next

field over, where families had booked sites well in advance and paid

a fee. But our spot was free: Allie and Reese's Tahoe, was parked

neatly under a large shade tree, big enough to accommodate my

Cherokee also, not that the sun was out in the early Oregon morning

with any intensity, but like the rest of the people in the path of

totality, I was keeping my fingers crossed that it would be, *soon*.

Showtime was 9:05:42 a.m. precisely, but for now, the sky was still

painted with early morning fog, something we hoped would

dissipate. It did. Happily, we watched the last cloud disappear by nine, and we watched the moon take its first bite out of the sun shortly after.

"I can't believe the moon is going to completely cover up the sun," Reese exclaimed, his voice sounding louder, as night fell around us, slowly, and revealing the excitement that all three of us felt.

"It's going to!" I felt like I was shouting, the world seemed to get smaller, making my words come out in rapid-fire. "Don't take your eclipse glasses off." I reminded both Allie and Reese, as I began to watch the sun disappear a sliver at a time through mine.

"I can't believe this." The exuberating surprise could be heard in Reese's declaration.

"Mom, it's like watching the world disappear." This time it was Allie. I was holding her hand, the three of us lying flat on a navy-blue comforter I had brought from home, and I could feel her body quiver with excitement, something I was feeling too, only mine came out in the form of tears, which I quickly dried with my free hand, keeping my eyes closed in a tight squinting position, to avoid any eye damage, as I disrupted the cardboard eclipse glasses that had been positioned on my face. "Are you okay Mom?"

"They're happy tears," I answered. Allie could sense my tears of awe, but was unable to turn her head, like all of us, focused on the disappearing sun, and still holding onto each other, as the world appeared to come to an end.

At 10:17:51 a.m. it did, for three members of the Sinaloa Cartel, known drug traffickers, the very reason Aaron Bosman worked his way up in the ATF office, and the very reason he lost both of his parents when he was a fifteen, innocent victims of a road rage shooting, on Alameda Street, an area known for violence, the Rancho Dominquez area, part of Compton, an even smaller part of Los Angeles, and a landmine for unsuspecting tourists. Bosman never went a day in his life without thinking about the rare trip to Disneyland, a dream come true for an only child, especially one raised in a Jehovah Witness home. It was a day that Bosman would carry in the pit of his stomach into adulthood, constantly suppressing the urge for revenge; instead, he would become a dedicated civil servant; but now, things had changed, and even though time had passed, the cancer in the Rancho Dominquez neighborhood was still spreading like wildfire. Drugs. Rape. Murder. A continuous cycle. *If I can just get two or three of them before they take me out.* Aaron thought as he pulled up to the Sky Exotic Cabaret, a well-known topless bar that was frequented by the Sinaloa Cartel, minutes before opening hours, giving the drug runners a chance to be with the ladies, the ones who wanted extra money. The cops knew about the activities before, during, and after hours. Hell, the place was always under surveillance, but rarely busted. The police, turned a blind eye, letting them live in their hell; but today, Aaron Bosman would join them. He had done his own long-distance surveillance on the cartel throughout the years, pulling rap sheets, memorizing faces, and getting the inside scoop, even 2,300 miles away. As Associate Deputy Director of the ATF office in Detroit, he had eyes everywhere, just by making a phone call. It was now or never. Today, he would use his non-dominant hand, once again. His successor's belief in the Harvard research was right. He had plenty of time to think about it, first driving there, then paying the ten-dollar cover charge, then standing inside, long enough to select his targets, men he recognized, men he was certain were part of the Sinaloa Cartel. Then, as Los Angeles experienced a seventy-percent blockage of the sun, the city too far south to be in the path of totality, he pulled out his .38 special, and fired three rapid shots – POW,

POW, POW – one at each pre-selected target. He hit the ground, just as his third bullet entered his final target's skull. Aaron Bosman wouldn't become one of the 144,000 people to enter heaven, neither would the three dead drug runners.

#

It was at that very moment, eighty-seven of them if seconds are moments, that Enola May Starks, removed her eclipse glasses. She could feel the tiny hairs on her arms tingle, a reaction to the temperature-drop over the last hour, and had heard the sound of night crickets in the open field. Now, time stood still. For eighty-seven seconds. They were caught in a time warp. A total solar eclipse. Enola watched the blackened sky hover over the sleeping meadow. Her reaction was to not move. She mustered the strength to whisper to the side of Allie's face.

"I love you." She could still smell the faint scent of coconut, even now, in Allie's hair, from the last shampoo. "You must own stock in coconut." Enola joked. "So do I." She thought about how much alike they sometimes were, right down to shampoo scents.

"Coconut?" Allie laughed at her mother's attempt at humor, at a time when she questioned whether the world was over. "We're lying in total darkness, and all you can think of is coconut?" Allie's tiny frame bounced in laughter. "Mom, the world is ending!" She announced, just as a Willamette Mission State Park employee, used a microphone, to make an announcement to the viewers.

"Okay, here we go again folks. Put your eclipse glasses back on."

Enola watched Allie and Reese place their glasses back on, then quickly followed suit, before the world slowly started to return, and before responding to Allie's last proclamation.

"No, it's not ending." She squeezed Allie's hand. "It's beginning all over again." She didn't realize how accurate that statement would become.

The End